TEN AVATARS

Shahana Dattagupta

Flying Chickadee Creations

ISBN 978-0-578-04971-7

First printing, March 2010

Flying Chickadee Creations

PO Box 30021, Seattle, WA 98113-0021

www.flyingchickadee.com

"The Dollhouse" was originally written for and presented at *Yoni ki Baat*, Seattle, 2008.

Original art "Cracking India," and cover design by Shahana Dattagupta

Copy editing and proof-reading by Shirin Subhani and Parijat Nandi

Author photograph by Jason J. Week

In loving memory of "mashi" –
Prof. Meenakshi Mukherjee;

For all those years of love and family,
and for saying to me again and again:
"Write, Munna, write."

In ancient Hindu mythology, **Avatar** or **Avatāra** (Sanskrit for "descent") refers to the intentional descent of a deity from heaven to earth. Vishnu, a male deity and the "preserver" in the holy trinity of Hinduism, was said to have ten avatars. Avatar is commonly translated into English as "incarnation," but more accurately as "appearance" or "manifestation." In a more abstract, modern-day use, avatar could connote an embodiment or personification, as of a principle, attitude, or view of life. Here, ten avatars of woman are explored in vignettes of the Indian-American experience.

There was never yet an uninteresting life. Such a thing is an impossibility. Inside of the dullest exterior there is a drama, a comedy, and a tragedy.

Mark Twain

To live is so startling it leaves little time for anything else.

- Emily Dickinson

And in the end, it is not the years in your life that count. It is the life in your years.

- Abraham Lincoln

* * * * *

If my doctor told me I had only six minutes to live, I wouldn't brood. I'd type a little faster.

- Isaac Asimov

Contents

1

The Goddess

Durga! Dooorgaaa! Mother was calling from the kitchen. *Oh my goodness; somehow Mother must know.* She was playing with make-up at Mother's dresser, painting her lips a violent red and her eyes a jet black. Durga stared in the mirror in horror. Then she quickly wiped her mouth on the back of her shoulder, smearing her yellow frock's sleeve with smudges of crimson, before Mother could spot the forbidden activity. Durga now had an exaggerated appearance, with protracted eyes and mouth, red and black lines streaking to the edges of her face. *Where is your sister?* Mother stormed into the bedroom, and glared down at the wide-eyed, sloppy-lipped, little girl. Durga shook her head. *Aren't you supposed to watch her? Aren't you the Big Sister? God, these children ... one day, you will all know when I'm gone ...* Mother stomped off angrily, grumbling and muttering, in search of Sister. Durga heaved a sigh of relief; at least she had escaped Mother's attention, and possible punishment for the smeared lipstick.

Durga often wondered what Mother meant by *being gone*. When Grandfather had disappeared from his hospital bed, Mother had explained that sometimes people go away, to a place in the Heavens, above the big white clouds. Unfortunately, once they go there they never return. Durga still remembered Grandfather in his dirty-green clothes, lying motionless on the white bed, plastic tubes slipped in and out of his nose and mouth. Grandfather never returned, and his picture now hung on the wall with a garland of yellow flowers strung limply around the frame. Grandmother now dressed in a plain, white sari, and sobbed late into the night on the dark verandah of their upper-story flat in Calcutta, where the large crows flocked in the day, cawing relentlessly and threatening to mercilessly peck people hard on the head. Fear gripped Durga's heart with a tight fist when Mother threatened to be gone. The clouds looked like a lovely place, but what if Mother never returned too? Durga made a habit of sneaking into her parents' bedroom at night, to check if Mother was still breathing. She knew they disliked it, especially Father. Sometimes the bedroom door was locked shut. On these nights Durga panicked outside, her ear pressed to the door. Maybe Mother was going away. Maybe Father was making her go away. Durga waited and waited, till somehow, the door opened, and then she curled up at Mother's and Father's feet to keep vigil. Or sometimes, she fell asleep on the clammy terrazzo floor outside the locked bedroom door.

Mother was still muttering, now back in the kitchen, Sister at her side. Sister was being forced to drink from the hot tumbler of milk, which was compulsory in the mornings and late afternoons. Durga had already drunk hers. It was never quite clear to Durga what Mother muttered under her breath. Or why she seemed so angry and tired all the time. Mother sweat in the kitchen, with beads of perspiration running down like rivulets along the sides of her face, and then stood under the ceiling fan turned on full, with her hands on her hips. She took big gulps from tall glasses of water, and Durga could see through the bottom of the glass, her teeth mysteriously grow larger in the water, like shiny-white, floating fangs. In the evenings Mother showered, and then stood under the fan again, combing her hair, her neck and armpits lined with white furrows of talcum powder. Then she lit an incense stick and waved it in front of the Goddess's picture on the wall. Grandfather's picture, a smaller version of the garlanded one in Grandmother's house, was also next to Goddess's. Sometimes Mother replaced the water in the silver cup she kept in front of Grandfather, on a little shelf. Durga kept a regular watch on the water in the cup to see if Grandfather was really drinking it; the level did seem to go down over time. If Durga was in the room, Mother asked her to fold her hands as well. After all, she was a gift from the Goddess at the end of all those difficult, toiling years in America, wasn't she? She was even named after the Goddess! Durga peered through half-closed eyes at her divine namesake in awe; with her ten hands looming over her head, each armed with a different, gleaming weapon, and her third eye piercing and fierce, the Goddess looked like she knew all about Durga's clandestine make-up sessions.

Grandmother, before Grandfather had gone away to the clouds, had told her all about Goddess Durga. When Demon Mahisha had struck evil on Earth, and no God could defeat his terrorizing rampage, the Gods had to hatch a special plot to destroy him. This Demon had once performed a severe penance, and had been granted an immunity boon by the very same Gods: no man could kill him! So, when Mahisha had become out of control, the Gods had to convene and conspire to get around the boon, and they had finally come up with an idea: they could create a female power to destroy him instead! They had convinced Lord Shiva's wife, Parvati, to be incarnated as a female savior on Earth. So, the form of Durga had been created with ten hands, and every one of the important Gods had donated their signature weapon to each of her hands. The Goddess had then descended on Earth riding her animal vehicle, the valorous Lion – as fierce and powerful as Durga herself – and she had pierced her wrathful trident straight through Mahisha's heart.

Soon after her shower Mother usually prepared some tea, and paced up and down the hallway until Father returned from work. Father put down his black office-bag, and Sister ran into his arms. Later, Mother and Father sat together in the two living room cane chairs, drinking tea and eating salted crackers. Father told Mother about his day, and Mother complained how bad the children had been all day. Sometimes Father was affectionate in spite of Mother's complaints, especially to Sister; sometimes he scolded them for their abominable behavior. Durga loved to hear Mother and Father talking, especially when they used big words like that. About all those people at Father's office, about the neighbors, about Mrs. Murty who lived near the health-center, about the grocer who stopped by, and about Eldest Aunt's letter with the latest family news. While Sister talked softly with her pillows in the bedroom, Durga stood around the doorway, just out of sight, straining to hear every word they said. Often their voices started out warm and friendly, but eventually got loud and argumentative. Then Durga's stomach churned. She knew exactly what would happen next: Father would yell, Mother would sob and the good times would be over. *Your Father is a demon! He's going to kill me! Do you know how he left me stranded in the streets of New York?* Mother would hiss through her teeth. There would be silence over dinner, and Durga and Sister would be ordered to bed immediately afterwards. Durga would have to lie awake, waiting to walk over in the darkness to make sure Mother was breathing, make sure Father was not making her go away.

The Goddess

Sometimes Mother took them to the park in the hot afternoons after school. *Wear your hats or you'll get a sunstroke*, she screamed. All the children in the park waited their turn at the swings. Sister was always allowed first when a swing came empty. Mother provided the necessary push every time the swing returned, keeping Sister giggling in perpetual motion, just like the brass pendulum in the huge clock in Neighbor's house. When another swing was empty, Durga sat herself in it and swung her legs out with all her might. She was the Big Sister, wasn't she? She knew how to swing herself! She checked sideways from time to time to see if she was going as far into the skies as Sister. Oh, a few more inches, and she would be there! Durga loved the warm breeze skimming her ears with a whoosh-whoosh sound. Always too soon for Durga, Mother signaled to leave. Sometimes Durga sat in the sand and kicked her legs – she did not want to go home – a fresh batch of older kids had just arrived. But Mother always prevailed and Sister always obeyed. Durga eventually had to follow, or Mother dragged her along by the arm, carrying Sister sideways on her hip.

Some other afternoons when Mother was in a better mood, she took out the thick album with photos of Mother and Father after they had eloped and moved to America in 1968. On later pages there were pictures of Durga when she was just a baby. Mother looked lovely in the photos, and Durga leaned forward eagerly to find the sparkle in her dark eyes. *See that one? You were only a day old, and they just loved you in that Pittsburgh hospital because you had so much thick, black hair even as a newborn!* Durga had these stories memorized, but she loved it when Mother told them to her all over again. The story of how the doctors brought her out of Mother's tummy with a long cut, for which Mother had to be unconscious for some time. The story of her annaprasan ceremony, the first time she had eaten grown-up food. An Indian Uncle, a colleague from Father's Chemistry Department, had fed her the first morsel. Traditionally, Mother's brother

– Older Uncle – would have done the honors, but how was he to be there in America, all the way from Calcutta? And later, how Durga had wanted to only eat spicy Indian fare, refusing her mushy American baby-food, and demanding spiced eggs and rice in American friends' homes. And how she had made ice-creams in the snow by sticking snow balls on fallen twigs. And the story of how Mother had to run really fast with baby Durga in a pram because a policeman was chasing her. He had mistaken the red dot on Mother's forehead for blood, and had only wanted to help her! The story of Durga's running a fever of 105, and being placed in a refrigerated chamber by smart American doctors. And then, when Father got his first job offer in India as a young scientist, and Mother had a big belly with Sister inside, how they had left their life in America to return to their home country, unlike any of the other Indians they knew. And the story of how their plane back to India hadn't taken off in time because of Durga's life-size, realistic, black doll, which the stewardess had mistaken for an extra passenger! When Mother told these stories and flipped the pages of the album, her voice had a rare, fleeting joy in it, and Durga held on to every word and every moment with rapture and glee.

But Mother really seemed happiest when Postman knocked on the door in the afternoons and delivered a letter with family news. Was it Eldest Aunt's, or Middle Aunt's? *Youngest Aunt was soon to be married*, the letter said. *They had finally found her a good husband. Even Younger Uncle was returning from abroad for the wedding.* Mother said they were all to board the air-conditioned train, and travel across the country to Calcutta for the wedding. Durga was thrilled; she would soon wear her blue satin-and-lace dress, and maybe even put on lipstick like Older Cousins! There would be lots of grown-ups talking and cheering in their confident voices, and Durga would feel safe. *Everyone knew how happy Grandfather would be today if he were alive.* Mother's lips trembled as she read through the lines of writing on the fluttering blue paper, the words blotting through the back; but in all, she seemed pleased. Durga sat sprawled on the floor next to her, very happy to see Mother smiling.

Some evenings Father's colleagues visited for tea, snacks, and a chat. That always made Father happy and Mother nervous. *Were there enough biscuits in that rippled glass jar?* Sometimes they came with their wives and children. The children were sent away to the bedroom to play with toys. But the laughter and merriment in the grown-ups' chatter was a much greater lure for Durga. While Sister generously showed the other children all her toys, Durga took her usual post around the doorway, her ear glued to the lively conversation. Sometimes Mother spotted her nearby, and asked her to carry the tray of biscuits into the living room. At these times Durga liked to steal the opportunity to stay longer and swallow every word uttered. Maybe one of the Uncles would show her a trick, or one of the Aunties would ask her to sing a song. But Mother was quick to catch on. *Go inside, Durga, and play with the other children!* Durga left hesitantly, and quietly resumed her guard at the wall-corner. Oh, why was she not a grown-up? Why did she have to play silly games with the other children? How long did she have to wait to be an adult? *You're only five-and-a-half years old!* Mother usually scolded. *Behave like a child!* Durga was puzzled; how was she to be Big Sister and Child at the same time?

On Sunday mornings Father sat in the cane chair and read the thick newspaper. Durga stirred in her sleep in the early morning, comforted to hear the happy crackling of the newspaper pages, and the voices of Mother and Father wafting through the walls, lulling her back to sleep. After multiple rounds of tea, Mother prepared a special breakfast, either of savory potato pancakes, or sweetened cream-of-wheat with raisins, or a sago pilaf. Mother looked generally happy, the beads of sweat on the sides of her face glistening with joy. There were other Sunday mornings, however, that were vastly different. The wafting voices grew louder and sharper, the newspaper fell with a smarting slap to the ground, and Durga sat up in terror. ...*You never stop repeating that!* ... *Who asked you to run along with me, anyway?* ... Father's voice shouted. Mother's laments were muffled between sobs ... *Oh, what a mistake I made ... Oh, when I'm gone* ... On those days there were no multiple rounds of tea. Or pancakes, or sweet semolina. Mother shuffled through the hallway, tears mixing with sweat on her cheeks, a ghoulish look in her eyes, and she locked herself in the bedroom. Father silently picked up the newspaper again, or fetched himself some dry bread and a banana. Sister was still asleep in her crib. Durga lay awake, waiting for Mother to open the door again, and hoping desperately that there was no secret door leading from the locked bedroom to the place in the clouds.

This evening Durga had resumed playing with the make-up in Mother's dresser. She had painted her lips again, and was working around her eyes with the black kohl pencil. Sister was quietly playing with her toys in the other room. Father was not home yet; he was late. Mother had made tea a whole hour ago, and was pacing faster and faster in the hallway, sweating from the effort. As soon as Father walked in, Mother grumbled and asked questions. Father's voice was low at first, but soon he started to yell. Mother began to cry. Father's words got louder, and Mother's sobs got deeper. Mother's shrill voice rang out occasionally, and soon Father's footsteps were thumping on the floor. Their words were no longer clear, but merely garbled noise that made Durga's head swim round and round, much like an extended session on the swings made her feel.

Durga stared in the mirror in terror. Then she saw Goddess's all-knowing third eye watching her from the wall. Durga painted a third eye on her forehead with the kohl, gleaming and glistening in her reflection. Now she could hear trumpets and horns blowing around her, the Gods calling to her, preparing her for battle with great fanfare. Her ten hands were stretched out like a peacock's fan around her body, and the Gods were arming them one by one: a club here, an axe there, a spinning disc in the next ... and finally, the grand trident. Lion was waiting, his mane glowing in its golden glory, his whiskers twitching, and his tail swishing in anticipation. With intention in her mind and power in her arms, Durga descended on Earth, her long black hair flying wildly around her face, and her eyes dark with quiet, purposeful anger. She stomped about in search of Mahisha. In her present incarnation, Durga's head almost touched the ceiling fan under which Mother often stood to dry her sweat and tears, and she now stood towering over Father. Father appeared small and powerless as he knelt in front of Durga, weeping and begging for forgiveness. But Durga was determined; she was going to show no mercy whatsoever. Mahisha was making Mother cry. Mahisha was making Mother go away. Mahisha had to be punished.

2

The Politician

The pain in Mallika's head was excruciating. The migraines had recently become less frequent, but when one did strike, it did so with a deadly vengeance, as if compensating for the longer hiatus. The Ambassador taxi violently swerved left and right, tooting its horn loudly, skirting ditches, pedestrians, cows, bicyclists, motorbikes, and large, ambling buses overflowing with people. With each vigorous jerk or deafening honk the pain was amplified in Mallika's skull, and the vomit poked in her throat, ready to gush through her mouth any moment. In the worn and ratty backseat of the cab, Mrs. Sengupta sat next to her, holding on tight, throwing anxious glances her daughter's way and asking every few minutes, "Do you need some lavang?" "Shall I roll down the window?" There was no telling if the heavily polluted Delhi air would make things any better, or much worse. Mallika wished her mother would just leave her alone, at least until this harrowing cab ride was over, and they were at the Hazrat Nizamuddin railway station. *This isn't a good start*, she thought. She had honestly intended this trip to Udaipur as a treat for her mother, making an earnest bid to spend some quality, one-on-one time together, but things were already starting out on the familiar, contentious note. Mallika grabbed the bottle of water next to her, and rapidly swallowed two Aleve from the little pill-holder she had brought back with her from the U.S. Even through the waves of pain, a little smile broke from her lips; she remembered the time Andy had given her the little container, on an evening she had swung by his place after class. Sweet, considerate Andy.

After what seemed like eons to Mallika's screaming head, they pulled up in front of the railway station. There was the usual bickering with the taxi driver about money owed, followed by swarms of red-uniformed coolies who appeared like flies around honey, vying for attention and asking to carry the luggage to the right train for a nominal fee. In her early years of return visits to India Mallika had held on stubbornly to her newfound American independence, gruffly shooing off the coolies, finding the display board in the main hall to locate her train, and dragging her luggage up and down the various overpasses to find her train. On her last trip, however, she had become savvier, convinced that *When in Rome do as the Romans do* was one of the wisest idioms ever coined. Besides, the coolies often had information that wasn't yet on the displays. She had learned to use her instincts to quickly pick out a face from the yelling bunch – like choosing the best puppy out of a litter – and just run with him. Besides, today she was in such pain that she couldn't imagine carrying anything up and down the stairs anyway. Beating her mother to the negotiations, Mallika selected a coolie, set a rate, and soon, they were weaving their way through the thick crowd – beggars, children, dogs, vendors – and all the sights, sounds and smells that can only be encountered, in the whole world, at an Indian railway station. It's why Michael, Mallika's American brother-in-law, liked to stand at these railway platforms and inhale deeply. "This is where you see real life," he often declared, heroically opting to travel in the second class, non-air-conditioned cars, in order to fully experience India.

Their train was already deployed to its platform. The beads of sweat glistened on Mrs. Sengupta's face and neck as she hustled along to keep pace with her daughter and the coolie. Quickly locating their names on the list outside the air-conditioned, two-tier car before her mother could get any more flustered, Mallika jumped into the train, and extended a hand. Their coolie was ahead of them, already scoping out their seats, and setting down their luggage to mark territory. While Mallika settled fees with him, Mrs. Sengupta entered what appeared to be their four-berth cabin, and looked instantly distressed. Their tickets said they had seats B-12 and B-13, then how come this man in an impeccably starched white dhoti was blissfully recumbent on one of their berths? Promptly, and before Mallika could investigate how the berth numbering worked, Mrs. Sengupta pounced on the man. "This is *our* seat!" she declared loudly in Hindi, a concoction of confidence and indignation lacing her voice. The man looked up slowly and deliberately from his newspaper, his glasses balanced at the tip of his nose, and at first, said nothing. Mallika took a rapid look around and realized that B-12 was actually paired with B-11 across the aisle, where two berths were stacked opposite the four-berth cabin, but of course it was too late. Mrs. Sengupta had already attacked the man, and he was now gazing steadily at both of them, sizing them up, reflecting on either the most deserving response, or whether they merited one at all. Finally he spoke in a low but deep voice. Firmly and unequivocally, and in crisp tones of Hindi, he stated, "No. This berth is mine." That's it, end of story. Mrs. Sengupta stood speechless. She looked stunned; she was accustomed to being Headmistress and issuing commands in various high schools, yet *she* had just been spanked for misbehavior in the Principal's office! Mallika didn't know whether to be embarrassed, or amused. Motioning her mother to take B-13 within the more comfortably ensconced four-berth cabin, she sat down across the aisle in B-12, and rested her head against the window. It was a relief to finally have a few stationary moments, and allow the drugs to kick in before the train began its journey.

Mrs. Sengupta, however, was not in the least satisfied with this arrangement. She leaned over, projecting her voice across people and their coolies walking up and down the aisle in search of their seats, trying to get Mallika's attention. "But how can we travel like this? Poor you, you have a headache, and all these people are going to knock your feet and arms all night long as they walk by in the aisle!" she exclaimed in their mother-tongue Bengali. Mallika struggled to maintain her cool. "Ma, please just settle down. It's OK, I just need some quiet; I cannot talk much right now. When the medicine takes effect everything will be fine. *I will be fine.*" Mallika added extra emphasis to the last part of her response, but Mrs. Sengupta wasn't having any of it. Motherly concern was only partly at play; what was really bothering Mrs. Sengupta was that things weren't as she had expected or imagined, that they were presently outside her control. She felt cheated. Her daughter was sitting outside her immediate purview, and she had to travel facing this weird, rude man, who had so callously dismissed her!

Across the aisle, Mallika was keenly aware that Mr. White Dhoti, reclining in B-14, was observing the dynamics between Mrs. Sengupta and her daughter with shrewd, unwavering interest. He peered periodically over his glasses, just above the edge of his newspaper, and then went back to reading. Twice, his cell phone jingled in a tune vaguely familiar to Mallika, and he answered in his low, deliberate voice with almost regal command, "Jai Shri Ram!" It was clear that the ensuing conversation was, on both occasions, with someone subservient receiving instructions to be followed to the letter. Between throbs that were gradually receding in intensity, Mallika savored the pure, unadulterated Hindi rarely spoken these days. "Why didn't you get the papers to court in time?" A pause later, "Those, mister, are unacceptable excuses. I think you are quite capable of getting the needful done in two days. Two days, Suneel ji!" he ordered flatly, and hung up. Mallika turned her face away to the window, avoiding not only his gaze but also her mother's.

A vendor passed by, calling like a throaty toad on a wet night, "chai, chai, chai..." Mallika's own phone began to ring. It was her best friend Ranjana, checking to see if they had made it to the train alright. Ranjana had helped to plan the whole trip, making online train reservations on the new-and-improved Indian Railways website, as well as arranging a four-star hotel near the lake in Udaipur, since Mallika had insisted on pampering her mother. Mrs. Sengupta had clicked her tongue in protest, complaining that it was all much too expensive. It ran in her blood to covet the best of comforts, but worry and fret about the expense, unless someone thrice removed from the family was paying for it all. Mallika gave Ranjana a quick editorial of events thus far, leaving her giggling hopelessly on the other end. They had been friends since the age of twelve, and little needed to be said for everything to be understood. As Mallika hung up, she spotted four men, lanky but for their rice-fed potbellies, huddled in the aisle separating her from her mother. A black, medium sized bag and a water bottle were now sitting on the berth above Mr. White Dhoti, so it appeared that at least one of the men was going to be traveling in B-15. The men were laughing, slapping each other's backs and kidding in Bengali, and Mallika could see a familiar gleam in her mother's eyes; quickly and surely, a new scheme was hatching in her head. Before Mallika could abort it, Mrs. Sengupta was talking to the men in Bengali in her most plaintive voice, "Misters, which of you is traveling in this seat? You see, my daughter is way over there, across the aisle, and she is *so* unwell. Would you mind exchanging berths with her? It would be *so* kind!" Mallika shot big glares of protest her mother's way, but the lanky man in checkered pants was already saying, "Oh, of course, of course, mashima! No problem at all." Mallika felt Mr. White Dhoti's unflinching gaze even through all the chaos, and in a bid to assert her last shred of independence in his witness, she directly addressed Checkered Pants, "Thank you for your generosity, sir, but I am comfortable here for now. I will let you know later if I need to swap berths with you." With this, Mallika turned her face away once again and covered it with her scarf, shielding herself from all their stares. But even through the fabric she could feel the heat of her mother's disapproving eyes.

* * * * *

Mallika awoke with a start; the train was now happily chugging along. She glanced at her watch – it showed 7:45pm – so the train must have been moving for at least forty five minutes. It was now fully dark outside, and she could only see the occasional village light glowing like a firefly in the scale-less, black landscape. Checkered Pants's buddies had disappeared, and he was sitting next to Mrs. Sengupta, fiddling with his cell phone like a boy with his new toy, oily curls framing his bent head, and his belly sticking out ludicrously from his thin, hunched frame. Mr. White Dhoti was still supine, now reviewing what looked like official documents. Mallika's head seemed to have eased, and she closed her eyes again thankfully, cherishing the chug-chug of the train that she so loved. It reminded her of those long train journeys she used to take from Bombay to Calcutta with her mother and older sister Maneka, to see her grandparents, aunts, uncles and cousins. Both cities now bore their native names – Mumbai and Kolkata – and Mallika bristled; in an over-zealous attempt to obliterate colonial vestiges, a bit of her personal history had been snatched away by her own people. The memories of those summer months always brought back vivid, mixed feelings: the joy and security of the larger family network, but also the dark shadows of sickness that Calcutta had inevitably cast upon her, and Mrs. Sengupta's anxious fretting over every little thing ... Mallika's mind jumped abruptly to her present life in State College, Pennsylvania. Studying and teaching concurrently, living independently, going out for drinks, dinners and drives with Andy and their group of friends, shopping in the large, abundant malls and grocery stores, zipping off to New York or Washington D.C. or Philadelphia on the fast highways ... How different it all was from her life growing up in India, and how hard she tried to describe all the nuances to Andy. He had promised to visit India with her soon, and now she imagined him on this train, sitting across from her, his white skin and blue eyes standing out absurdly in the brown sea of people, his body swaying with hers to the train's chug-chug-chug ... "Malli! Malli!" Mrs. Sengupta was calling, having got wind of her daughter being awake, and Mallika's reverie was rudely broken. "Are you feeling better now?" she asked, and Mallika could see Checkered Pants shifting in his seat, anticipating that this might be his cue to be banished to the lesser berth. Mallika nodded, again acutely aware of Mr. White Dhoti's surveillance of the proceedings. "Want to eat dinner now?" Mrs. Sengupta frequently produced a barrage of questions, never caring to hear the answers to any; really, they were directives in disguise. She now rose from her seat, and to Mallika's horror, began moving Checkered Pants's belongings from his upper berth to Mallika's aisle-side, lower berth. Realizing that she wasn't going to win in public in the face of her mother's determination, Mallika stood up wordlessly, clenching her teeth. Checkered Pants, on the other hand, seemed happily compliant with Mrs. Sengupta's ways; all this probably even brought back fond memories of his own cloyingly meddlesome Bengali mother. And so, he accepted the moving of his things as loving, maternal overseeing, and obediently moved himself over to his newly assigned seat. Mallika muttered a quick thanks to him as they crossed each other in the narrow aisle, and landed hard on the berth next to her mother, who was already on to the next thing: dinner. She was unwrapping parathas and opening up a multilayered tiffin-carrier that contained egg curry, dal and potato-subzi in its three tiers.

Unexpectedly, Mr. White Dhoti sat himself upright. And then he spoke to them for the first time since he had successfully quelled Mrs. Sengupta's attempted coup. "You are Bengali, and there is no fish curry in your dinner?" he teased, once again in crisp, pure Hindi. Mallika managed a smile, but Mrs. Sengupta only grunted under her breath, unwilling to entertain overtures after having suffered defeat barely an hour ago. "It's probably time for my dinner too!" he added, and began to unwrap his own package of aloo-parathas, saag, spicy pickles, and sour yoghurt. On her trips back to India it struck Mallika how eating really was a collective experience; even on trains, it was unspoken code for strangers to spontaneously eat together, often breaking the ice in the process. Mallika chomped on her parathas, eggs, and potatoes, and across from her, Mr. White Dhoti smacked his lips and licked his fingers. Afterwards, he poured himself a huge tumbler of water, and then produced a second package of sweets, with pedas and son-papdis. "Why don't you have some?" he generously extended the colorful cardboard box towards mother and daughter. Mallika hesitated, though both sweets were her absolute favorites, but Mrs. Sengupta didn't waste a moment. Promptly, she sprang forward and grabbed a couple of each, handing her daughter a share. Mallika thanked Mr. White Dhoti, and bit into the son-papdi with relish. It had been so long since she had eaten one of these flaky, buttery things!

"So, for what purpose are you traveling to Udaipur?" Mr. White Dhoti now asked. It was as if the sharing of dessert had given him the license to begin making specific enquiries into their lives. "Oh, just some sightseeing and family visits," Mallika answered politely, hoping to keep it vague. Mr. White Dhoti's shrewd eyes quickly scanned her jeans-and-shirt attire, shoes, hair and accessories, and he asked, "So I take it you are visiting from America?" Mallika never ceased to be amazed at how people, especially salesmen in Delhi's streets and stores, could spot a US- or UK-return in a matter of seconds. ("Hey, you even *smell* different!" Ranjana had once explained.) "Yes, I am," Mallika replied, again trying to keep it brief but polite. "Ah, I see. What are you doing there?" Mr. White Dhoti was obviously not accustomed to doing anything on other people's terms, and he was not about to take a hint and halt his enquiries. At least he had wagered a smart guess that she was single, and hadn't asked the more stereotypical "What is your husband doing there?" "I am attending graduate school, working on a Masters degree in educational psychology." "Accha? Very good, very good!" Mr. White Dhoti seemed to approve. "So you like it in America?" he probed. "Yes, I do, and I also like it here," Mallika replied. "Hmmnnnn …" he became pensive, mysteriously choosing to end his investigation at this point.

Just then a man appeared from nowhere, and sat down next to Mr. White Dhoti. The man had brought paan for an after-dinner treat, and Mr. White Dhoti continued his spree of generosity, passing out one paper-wrapped triangle each to Mrs. Sengupta and Mallika. Mallika wondered who this new man was, and where he had been all this time. "Do you need anything else, Ramprasad ji?" he asked like only a dutiful servant would, also in the same shudh-Hindi. "Well, what time is the train stopping at Sawai Madhopur, and for how long?" Mr. White Dhoti enquired, his tone officious. "Just after 11:40pm, sahib, and it will stop there for about seven minutes." "Anything else, sahib?" Mr. White Dhoti shook his head, and the man made a small bow, and disappeared as suddenly as he had appeared.

"Hmmnnn ... Ramprasad ji," thought Mallika. She opened a novel she had brought along, but now it was her turn to undertake a close surveillance of this man from behind the pages of her book. His clothes were very traditional – cotton, embroidered kurta over his dhoti – but also impeccable in quality, pressed neatly and elegantly. He had an expensive, woven Kashmiri shawl draped around his shoulders. His hair was combed back and slick with oil, the fragrance of which she could faintly smell from this distance, and his hands were well-manicured. He wore a gold chain around his neck, with some Hindu deity dangling from it as a pendant; it was hard to tell whether it was Krishna or someone else. The stack of documents sat on his side. As Mallika conducted her examination as discreetly as she could, Mr. Ramprasad's cell phone rang again. "Haan, Jai Shri Ram! Really? Well, we must get a handle on this before the elections, Sharma ji. No, no, that simply won't do. Put your forces to work immediately, is that clear?" Suddenly, it hit Mallika. *Of course!* This man was a politician from the Bharatiya Janata Party, popularly called BJP, currently in power in the central government! Undoubtedly he held some important office too. He had the pure Hindi, the commanding phone calls, the lackey bringing him paan, the god-locket … how high up was he in the chain, anyway? Mallika wondered if her mother had any inkling of this man's stature, having coolly devoured his pedas, son-papdi and paan. But Mrs. Sengupta had nodded off against the window, so Mallika re-opened her novel, trying to divert her thoughts from the politician.

About an hour later Mr. Ramprasad got up and left the cabin. Moments after his exit the train stopped, and out of the pitch darkness Mallika could suddenly hear the growing roar of an approaching mob. Instinctively she became guarded, and shook her mother awake. As they listened to make sense of the sounds, four men with thick flower garlands wrapped around their arms barged into their cabin. Their eyes bulged with craze and they were practically falling over each other, panting heavily with excitement. One of them looked Mallika straight in the eye. "Where is Ramprasad ji?" he demanded, as if she were personally responsible for making him disappear. "I don't know, I think he went towards the toilets a few minutes ago," Mallika replied, her body tense and alert to the reeking of fanaticism. Outside, the mob had doubled its volume. The men with garlands left just as abruptly as they had appeared, and moments later, Mallika and her mother could hear the crowd shouting slogans and synchronized chants of "Jai Shri Ramprasad! BJP zindabad!" Another three minutes passed with the slogan shouting, and then the train began to slowly pull away. Mr. Ramprasad returned adorned with several garlands, rose petals in his now tousled hair, and a thick, orange tikka decorating his forehead, with his lackey in tow. Seeing the wide-eyed expressions on the faces of mother and daughter, he took off the garlands and set them aside dismissively, as if reassuring them that he was merely a co-passenger, a regular citizen, no more. The assistant took the garlands from him, and made a motion to leave. "Bring tea in the morning for these ladies, Mohan!" Mr. Ramprasad ordered. Mohan nodded, and discreetly disappeared. Mallika shuddered. It was time to climb up to the safety of her upper berth.

* * * * *

In the berth directly above Mr. Ramprasad, Mallika had spent a restless night, catching short bouts of sleep between alternately staring at the train's ceiling that hovered fifteen inches above her nose, and a heavily cob-webbed fan that hung from it. Now she was woken by "chai, chai, chai" calls, and quickly in the heels of this announcement, Mohan, Mr. Ramprasad's obedient assistant, showed up with two thermoses of tea and three ceramic cups. Mallika was impressed; this tea was delicately spiced with cardamom; it was not the sugar syrup that passed for chai on the trains. *Only the best for Ramprasad ji,* thought Mallika, but also for his co-travelers, who had been unexpectedly elevated to government-official status. She suspected that her mother was secretly relishing this status-by-association, especially as it came with quality tea to begin her morning, but wasn't about to admit it. Mallika had just taken a couple of sips when Mrs. Sengupta began motioning her to descend from her upper berth. "Arre,

Udaipur will be here soon; don't you want to come down and pack up your stuff?" There it was, another directive masquerading as a harmless question. Mallika hugged her knees stubbornly for a bit, then made her way down the ladder on the aisle-side, and swung over to sit sullen-faced next to her mother. She had clearly overheard a vendor say that Udaipur was a half-hour away, but knew well that her mother would not be in peace until she had fully staged their impending disembarkation. When the train finally pulled into Udaipur station a few minutes past 7am, they said hurried thank yous and good byes to Mr. Ramprasad, and left with a coolie.

Hailing a cab, Mallika and Mrs. Sengupta found their way to their grand hotel with lush, private gardens. The building had been a colonial residence during the British Raj, and still bore an air of regality. They were promptly offered freshly-squeezed fruit juice in the lobby, and Mrs. Sengupta gleefully sipped her pineapple juice while Mallika completed the check-in formalities. "Oh my goodness, what a place!" Mrs. Sengupta exclaimed with childlike delight when they opened the door to their room, encountering its full-width bay window with built-in seat, and its panoramic view of Lake Pichola and the famous floating Taj Lake Palace hotel. Mallika felt a sudden gush of affection and a gladness in her heart for having extended herself to make this trip with her mother. While she briefly lounged in the bay window, Mrs. Sengupta launched a meticulous reconnaissance of the perks of their room: super-sized towels, soft slippers, silky bathrobes, fragrant bath supplies, shimmering drapes. Tea was of utmost importance, so she quickly located the selection and contraptions provided, in anticipation of her afternoon cup. An orderly knocked on the door, and Mrs. Sengupta appeared officious accepting the day's newspaper and Udaipur city-guide that he delivered to her.

After hot showers in their state-of-the-art, marble-clad bathroom, they set out to explore this charming, fairy-tale city of lakes, floating palaces and surrounding mountains, all of which had earned it the label "Venice of the East." A winding drive took them past Lake Pichola into the narrow lanes densely populated with stores upon stores of bright, mirrored and patch-worked Rajasthani handicrafts. Mrs. Sengupta was in the process of wangling a deal for a mirror-covered, side-sling bag to send back for Maneka, when a large, decorated elephant approached them, swaying its hips amidst bicyclists and auto rickshaws, and the bargaining was overshadowed by this utterly magnificent sight. After a few gift purchases for her own friends back in State College, Mallika directed their cab driver to take them to the city palace complex, where the maharajah Udai Singh had once resided with his maharani, ruling over the Mewar kingdom. The slightly humid air was pleasant, and the expansive garden court welcomed them towards the entry of the imposing, grand stone palace. Looking like crawling ants in the distance, people were gathered on the colonnaded viewing platform all the way at the top, and Mallika felt a compelling wish to be instantaneously transported up there. But they did it as it should be done, exploring every room, gallery and viewport alongside sun-tanned foreigners, NRI tour groups with video cameras, rambunctious Indian families vacationing from all over the country, and the easy-to-spot, newly-wed couples with eager eyes and shyly linked arms.

The art and architecture were stunning. Walking through the cusped arches at each transition, Mallika and Mrs. Sengupta came upon room after room of different scale and character. The stone columns were intricate, and the cupolas over the lovely jharokhas shaded viewers as they gazed out to the various prospects. Finally they arrived at the grand, colonnaded terrace at the top, with its magnificent 360-degree view only befitting maharajahs. Just as they were adjusting their eyes to the city, its lakes and the mountains beyond, there was a burst of activity in one of the corners of the terrace. Several people were congregated around one person, and a large colorful umbrella bobbed up and down over this central figure like a dancing cupola. There were high-pitched calls of "Jai Shri Ram!" and Mallika's body froze from fresh, definitive memory. The crowd parted to allow a glimpse, and there he was, Mr. Ramprasad the politician! He was dressed in a fresh set of clothes, but they were, again, a crisply pressed kurta and dhoti, with a Jahar jacket layered on top. A freshly applied orange tikka decorated his forehead. Mallika grabbed her mother's elbow to turn them around for a hurried escape, but the contingent was already advancing towards them. The moment in which Mr. Ramprasad spotted Mallika and Mrs. Sengupta was distinct; his eyes lit up in recognition. Shoving aside his sundry followers, he joined his hands and lifted his elbows, raising the Namaste dramatically over his head. Taking long strides towards them in this posture, he boomed across the palace terrace, "Jai Shri Ram!" Knowing now that there was no way out, Mallika folded her own hands and said, "Namaste, Ramprasad ji." Mrs. Sengupta, in a rare display of solidarity with her daughter, followed suit. "You are here?" Mr. Ramprasad exclaimed the obvious in his characteristic Hindi. "Had you only told me that you were coming to this great palace this very morning, I would have sent a private car to your hotel to fetch you here!" he chided. "Oh, that's very kind, Ramprasad ji, but we've got ourselves a taxi for the day," Mallika said quickly, unsure of how to field this public display of familiarity and magnanimity. Those in the loyal entourage bore through Mallika and her mother with intense stares. Who were these women, who had won such high favor with their beloved neta? Why had they never seen them before? "What else are you visiting today?" Mr. Ramprasad demanded, as if their itinerary was now under his personal purview, since they had entered his political jurisdiction. "Oh, we're just going to Saheliyon-ki-Bari after this, and then we want to do some more shopping, and enjoy a traditional Rajasthani dinner. Tomorrow we will visit some family, and leave by the evening train," Mallika said, changing her tactic and opting for full disclosure, hoping that the brevity of their visit would stop Mr. Ramprasad from further plotting. "Really? I too am returning by tomorrow's train to Delhi!" he exclaimed. Mallika was beginning to regain her composure and even find all this rather amusing. Here they were, holding court in a maharajah's palace with a politician, while his followers gaped, open-mouthed. "In that case we may see you again on the train tomorrow!" she declared with a big smile and newfound confidence. "So we may! So we may!" Mr. Ramprasad chanted with pomp and grandeur as if granting them a boon, and strode away with a flourish. His men stood staring for a few moments before turning to follow their marching leader down the palace stairway.

* * * * *

It was 6:30pm, and they were at the train station once again. The second day in Udaipur had been rather different from the first one, spent mostly with Mallika's cousin's family. Mrs. Sengupta's sister's daughter, Renuka, had married into a conservative Rajasthani family, and she had just had her second baby. So, most of the day's excitement had centered around a traditional Rajasthani celebration welcoming the eight-day-old infant. Mallika had stared quietly at her cousin, a reputed orthopedic surgeon, now draped in full Rajasthani garb, heavily bejeweled with bright-yellow gold, red sindoor thickly streaking the parting in her hair. The baby lay bundled in her folded arms, and all the women sang folk songs and fussed around her with sweetmeats. Was this the same Renuka with whom Mallika had giggled madly in their teenage days, turning the pages of porn under a flashlight between the sheets? Now, boarding the train at the railway station and waving goodbye to her cousin and her husband, Mallika felt strangely disconnected from everything she had known so intimately in all the years of growing up. Mrs. Sengupta was yelling to her niece in Bengali over the heads of clambering passengers, "When will you two visit Delhi? Come soon, and bring both the girls!"

When the train began to pull away they took their seats, and Mallika leaned back in her berth, her mind drawing a blank.

Then suddenly she remembered: the politician! He should be on the train too! "I wonder where Mr. Ramprasad is!" she pondered aloud to her mother. "Oh my God, good he's not here!" Mrs. Sengupta responded, clearly having forgotten the possibility of running into the shrewd man for the third time in two days. But Mallika's curiosity got the better of her. She knew there were only two cars in the second class, air-conditioned category, and it wouldn't take much to find him. "I'm just going to take a quick look," she told her mother, and set off to scan their car. Not seeing Mr. Ramprasad anywhere, she crossed over the accordion-like articulation linking the neighboring car. Walking up and down the aisle, she found no sign of the politician or his lackey there either. As she made her way back, she spotted a uniformed man hanging out at the train's half-open doors, smoking and chatting with one of the other service attendants. Assuming he was either the Ticket Collector or his assistant, she asked him in Hindi, "Sir? Do you have a Mr. Ramprasad on your passenger list?" Mr. T.C. looked her up and down, and demanded, "Why? Is he your relative, or what?" "Well, he's a government official my mother and I met on the onward journey, and he was supposed to also return to Delhi on this train. I was wondering if I could say Namaste to him." Upon mention of a government official, Mr. T.C. looked suitably impressed, and instantly aligned with Mallika's cause. He reviewed his passenger list with meticulous care and proclaimed victoriously, "Ah! His name is here, sister, and he is on the bogie next to yours." "But I already looked there!" Mallika told him. "Oh, I see. Perhaps he got busy with his political meetings and missed the train, no?" Mr. T.C. offered dutifully. Mallika thanked him, and returned to her seat to find her mother unwrapping the rotis and subzi that Renuka's cook had packed for their journey. After dinner Mallika settled in to her novel, while Mrs. Sengupta got busy turning the pages of a magazine.

A couple of hours later the train stopped at Chittaurgarh. People were getting on and off, beggars were pleading at the windows, and vendors were advertising their chai, sodas, chips, cream crackers, and magazines; all this hustle-bustle reminded Mallika again of those childhood train journeys. On the few occasions that their father had extricated himself from his books and hand-done mathematical calculations to travel to Calcutta with them, he would get off at the stations to buy bananas, water and chai, and play the trick of going missing when the train was pulling out. Maneka and Mallika would be routinely fooled into believing that their father had been left behind, and just when big tears would begin to well up in little Mallika's eyes, he would appear in the cabin doorway, laughing. Sometimes he had an *Amar Chitra Katha* in hand for the younger daughter, and chocolate for the older one. Elated and relieved to have her father back, Mallika would then become absorbed in the collection of diverse and ancient illustrated tales from the Mahabharata, Ramayana, Jataka, Panchatantra, and the Bible. Mallika smiled fondly at the memory of Kalia, the forever-wise crow who had taught her many life-shaping morals, and the train began to move again.

This was the last major stop for the night, and newly embarked passengers settled into their berths. Mr. T.C. would be making his rounds shortly, after which everyone would go to bed. Just as Mallika was getting absorbed in her book, a familiar voice wafted through the aisle towards them, and her eye caught the edge of a crisp dhoti. She looked up and there he was, Mr. Ramprasad! "Jai Shri Ram! "How are you two ladies?" Behind him Mr. T.C. stood grinning. "As soon as Ramprasad ji boarded at Chittaurgarh, I let Sir know that this nice young lady had been enquiring after him. Ramprasad ji insisted on coming to see you himself!" he explained, very proud to have enabled this connection, and gained the favors of a powerful government official. "Yes, yes, thank you," Mr. Ramprasad waved him off, and Mr. T.C. disappeared discreetly. The berth across mother and daughter was vacant, and Mr. Ramprasad ceremoniously seated himself there. It was déjà vu; everything looked identical to their onward journey together.

"So, how was the rest of your time in Udaipur?" Mr. Ramprasad asked. Impressed by his generosity in coming to visit with them, Mallika told him about their various adventures, and he began to nod and smile. He almost seems huggable, she thought randomly. Even Mrs. Sengupta joined in the conversation, and everyone let down their guard. Soon Mr. Ramprasad was telling them about his life in Lucknow, where he had been a barrister for many years before joining the BJP. He regaled them with stories of this culturally rich city, telling them about his ancestors, the various crafts and trades, and the musical traditions. When Mallika asked him about his family, he even told them about his children, revealing that his twenty-three-year-old son was just starting out as a young lawyer. There was no explicit mention of his wife, but Mallika now imagined her as the omnipresent, quietly toiling, indispensable pillar of the family.

The conversation thus far had primarily involved Mallika, but now, Mr. Ramprasad suddenly singled out Mrs. Sengupta and addressed her directly. "So, Mrs. Sengupta, why don't you summon your daughter back to our great, honorable motherland?" he asked, pointing towards Mallika, reducing her without notice to a powerless minor regarding whom important decisions were going to be made by responsible adults. "Arre, Ramprasad ji, you know what happens when these children grow up! She is going to make her own choices. Who am I to interfere? Who is going to listen to me anyway?" Mrs. Sengupta said with a touch of self-pity and feigned resignation. Mallika shifted in her seat uncomfortably. "Besides, she seems to be happy there," Mrs. Sengupta conceded in partial defense of her daughter. "Is that so?" Mr. Ramprasad raised his eyebrows, now shifting his gaze once again to Mallika. "Sure!" she exclaimed and shrugged, the American gesture unexpectedly slipping out in defensiveness. "After all, the land that feeds and supports me presently is also my motherland. I am so lucky to have two!" she added, hoping that Mr. Ramprasad would let it go on this philosophical note. But the maternal metaphor was too attractive, too rich with possibilities, for him to back off and give up. "Oh no, no, no!" he persisted, wagging his plump index finger disapprovingly. "There is a big, big difference. The birthing mother is supreme. She has ultimate rights. She is the one who deserves your seva in her old age," he said righteously, titling his head in Mrs. Sengupta's direction, as if paying homage to her inevitable sacrifices as a mother. Clearly, he had no doubt that the manipulative pandering to maternal sentiments in Mrs. Sengupta's presence would earn him big points, and Mr. Ramprasad looked terribly pleased with himself.

But Mallika, in sudden God-sent vision, saw the path to victory. Having sensed the strong Hindutva leanings in every pore of this man's existence, she said, "But Ramprasad ji, our beloved Bhagvan Sri Krishna too had two mothers, didn't he? In our culture we do not distinguish between Devaki, who birthed baby Krishna, and Yashoda, who raised him into the savior of humanity, do we?" "In fact," she continued, "In Hinduism, don't we even revere Yashoda, the raising mother, as the supreme mother-ideal? Even all our songs and lores are in Yashoda mayya's praise!" Mallika's countenance feigned innocence, but her pupils radiated the gleam of victory, certain of the utter brilliance and invincibility of this move. Mr. Ramprasad stared at her long and hard, his previously friendly eyes now narrowed and wily just as they had been on their first encounter two days ago. "What we say and what we do are two different things," he stated in his ever-crisp Hindi, his voice deepening to a dangerous tone. Mallika was tempted to say, "Is that so?" to match Mr. Ramprasad's previous scorn, but she knew that like any first-rate politician, he recognized fully when he was beaten. And Mr. Ramprasad had just been beaten in his own game, using his very own rules. Little had he imagined that who he had taken for an Americanized upstart would know enough to wield as a weapon, the most pristine and unarguable of illustrative examples from Hindu philosophy! Without another word he stood up, shaking out the folds of his dhoti and smoothing his kurta as if this act of order might somehow salvage his dignity. Then he took on an air of distant indifference and said flatly, "It is late; I should be going." "Jai Shri Ram!" he saluted one last time and stomped out of the cabin.

Sporting a big, smug smile, Mallika made her bed for the night. Lying down, she fell asleep quickly and peacefully to the chug-chug-chug of the train, never waking up to Kota, Sawai Madhopur, Bharatpur ... not even to Mathura, the very place where Bhagvan Shri Krishna, her savior of the day, was said to have been born on a dark, stormy night to Devaki and Vasudeva.

3

This Day of Thanksgiving

The thick aroma of strong Turkish coffee forms a comforting envelope around me while I await my usual brunch plate. It is the morning of Thanksgiving, and having descended from my apartment in my sweats with a mixture of hope and disorientation, I am delighted to find the *Open* light glowing in the window of Café Elbasha. Ghareeb has greeted me with his usual *Hi babe* and a warm hug, and has then disappeared behind the counter to prepare my meal. I have told him the usual *make me whatever you want Gary*, instead of picking from his delightfully eclectic menu of Palestinian, Turkish, Greek, and Italian delicacies. I started this practice since I discovered that Ghareeb often quietly makes himself some rare breakfast item from his mother's repertoire, which cannot be found on the menu. *Make me what you want* has become our secret code for *I want whatever you're having*.

I have now found my favorite spot in the corner of this charming café, at the last table by the piano and the large painting, and also right by the windows, on to which big drops of rain are splattering loudly. I love setting my purse down on the old piano bench, and sitting with my feet up on the chair's edge and my knees tucked under my chin, facing the rest of the café, ostensibly immersed in my reading but keeping a keen watch for all the regulars who come through. The couple (who think they are) in love forever, with intertwined fingers and matching coffee orders. (This is Seattle after all; there are infinite variables that make up an individual's coffee order.) The family with two young children, with whom Ghareeb loves to play. The old woman strolling in on a walker, whom Ghareeb unfailingly addresses as *Princess*. The man with the wild, long hair and lithe body movements, most certainly a painter or musician. The red-haired, young woman with tattoos and piercings, who is unflappably cheerful. The characters are as varied and distinct as their coffee preferences. Over time I look up less from my reading because I have learned to recognize each of them by their voice, gait or coffee order. Now and again I encounter surprise entrants, and then, I assess them and their likely life stories.

Six months ago it had seemed as if I would succumb to asphyxiation on weekend mornings. The weariness from yet another week of barely keeping it together at work would give way, upon awakening on Saturday mornings, to an enormous, overwhelming emotional deluge. I would lie in bed staring at the high ceiling of my tiny downtown studio, faced with a relentless landscape of silence, promising nothing but screaming ghosts of my past over the next forty eight hours. I didn't know which I abhorred more: the numb, rote nature of the workweek's structure that unfailingly brought forth my first-born functionality (*Oh Leela, what an amazing job you're doing despite all that you're going through!*), or the abrupt fluidity of the weekends that made no demands on me, allowing the staggering pain to bubble up and surface like oozing lava from the deep of my entrails. Then one morning I had dragged myself out of bed, and tumbled into the café at the street corner, tears forming a gag at the base of my throat in stubborn refusal to gush from my exhausted eyes, pink and burning from crying the night before. I am not quite sure at what point in time Ghareeb's brunch had become my weekend ritual, his café my living room, and Ghareeb and his brother Mahmud, my extended family.

I sit huddled in the corner, browsing through a day-old copy of the Seattle Times. There has been a hitch with the monorail. Somewhere in a remote Washington town a man has died while attempting sex with a horse. The neighborhood of Ballard is battling an invasion by condominium developers. Various counties have differing interpretations of the soon-to-be-implemented, no-smoking restriction within twenty-five feet of habitable spaces. Etherea Salon is having a red dress party. And huge numbers of poor, hapless people in New Orleans are still wading through the disastrous waters of Hurricane Katrina. I look up and see that a man has stumbled into the café. He is in rags, and drags along some semblance of luggage: a lifetime's belongings, perhaps. He seats himself at one of the nearby tables, and the stench of poverty engulfs me, valiantly trouncing the aroma of high-quality coffee. Mahmud emerges from behind the counter, and has a very, very quiet conversation with the man. Even from two tables away, it appears that nothing has been said at all. A few minutes later the man gets up silently and stumbles back outside, into the rain. Ghareeb soon brings out to me, eggs with feta cheese and peppers, two falafel made with ground parsley in the mix, a side of freshly made hummus, a bowl of sweet basha rice, and a cup of cardamom tea. I look up, and unexpectedly, a deep gratitude gushes to my eyes that cannot be verbally communicated, but Ghareeb looks at me like he knows.

It is now just over three months since the legal divorce. The memory of that time, waiting in the King County courtroom, is at once immediate and distant. The experience was oddly similar to standing in line at the returns-counter of a store. You are, say, at IKEA, the popular home furnishings store. Throngs of families stroll through variegated vignettes of home life, all glorious in their maple-fabric-color-and-light character. You are entirely convinced that normal families live blissfully in these pleasantly easy, geometric and colorful configurations. Hundreds bump into you in their avaricious seeking, but you don't mind because this is a collective experience, as if assembling together at God's door, at the Mecca of family living. Then suddenly, one of the furniture items you acquired doesn't assemble quite right. You are now in the returns area, a poorly-lit, cheaply-tiled box next to the parking lot, drafts of cold air sending chills up your spine while you wait in line with a cheap-paper number chit between your fingers. By the time your turn arrives, you are subliminally aware of the thick air of disapproval by some invisible public body screaming its collective judgment: *Leela, you fucked up.*

And so there I had stood, in line at the King County courthouse. *May I return this 8.5-year marriage and have my money back please? It doesn't work very well.* The judge, a crusty, expressionless man, had been all but falling asleep behind the counter in the little courtroom. After an oath, and six questions to which the right answers were no more complicated than a monosyllabic *Yes* or *No*, he had stamped my documents with a bang and pronounced somnolently: *Your marriage is now dissolved.* Just like that. It had taken precisely four minutes, hardly representative of the gravity of the situation. I had turned somewhat delirious, an enormous, simultaneous welling of tears and giggles threatening to gush out, but I had made a concerted effort to maintain courtly decorum. Eight hundred people in their heaviest silks and glittering jewels had been present to celebrate the union of two individuals in typical Indian extravaganza, on a wintry Delhi night. Nearly nine years later, a lawyer and I had taken a ten-minute walk for a four-minute appearance that had made possible a different kind of transition for me. There was, for this event, no question of publicly sanctioned celebration. Nearly a decade of my life was now appropriated as a sheaf of documents, enveloped in a manila folder in the archives of an American courthouse.

My daydream is broken by a new arrival. This time it is a toothless drunk, and she is making unintelligible, gurgling noises. It appears that she wants to use the restroom. Ghareeb hands her a key, perhaps in the spirit of the holiday; typically, a purchase is warranted for the use of the facilities. I watch from the corner of my eye as she emerges from the restroom and lingers uncertainly, surveying a platter of baklava with vague interest. Again, she makes garbled sounds. This time Mahmud asks her if she wants anything, and now she looks angry. I am alarmed, and want to hide my face in the paper. Some free association with the glint in her eye has jogged a remote, gnawing uneasiness. Then I know what it is: it is my dream from last night. In it, I am somewhere in India, in an old courtyard house with thick walls and a high plinth, and the air inside carries the dampness of age and history. I am hiding in the hallway with an acute urgency to escape to the outside world, but my feet are solidly glued to the cold floor; I do not want to leave behind my photographs. *My photographs! I must have my photographs!* I manage to creep stealthily through the dusty corridors of the house to gather the photographs in a little cloth sack, and I am about to spring to my escape when Rajiv emerges as an apparition from the traditional kitchen, where he has been drying dishes with a red gamchha. In response to his query I inform him that I am going out on a stroll. He says, *are you really?* The rag is slung over his shoulder as he approaches me, and before I know it, it is against my throat, now transformed into ice-blue blotting paper like from my school days. I see the glint in his eyes, but I am still in disbelief about what it means. Then in slow motion his other hand, holding a small kitchen knife, makes its way up to my throat. This is when I had woken up, screaming. Now I tremble from the memory, and I'm not sure if the babbling, haggard woman has sensed my alarm. She throws a wrathful look my way, and then makes a sudden exit into the wet street.

My therapist tells me it can take a long, long time. To leave behind those violent ghosts from my past, that is. The repeated nightmares with graphically depicted marital violence – some exaggerated from what really happened – leave me exhausted in the mornings, although I never remember them immediately upon waking. It is usually sometime later in the day, or even later in the week that I remember, when something else triggers a memory. And as if being exorcised from the annals of my unconscious, a gradually emerging picture of the nightmare completes into vivid form. It is as if I am living the violence three times over: once when it actually happened, once in my fretful sleep months afterward, and once again in my waking consciousness days thereafter. My therapist says that this is the human brain's way of processing trauma, bringing it forth from the unconscious to the sub-conscious, and then to the conscious. They call it post-traumatic stress-disorder. To cerebrally inclined people like me, it does help to explain phenomena such as these. In a way I am fascinated: I am at once protagonist and observer in this unfolding drama.

I don't quite know what to tell my parents, friends, and other well-wishers, who call from far-and-wide, asking how I am. Which nightmare do I recount? The one that actually happened? The one my brain dreams up at night? The one that torments me in broad daylight? How do I describe the constant, debilitating body-ache, the clenching in my gut, the sinking in my heart? I used to think that was a figure of speech, until now; I have literally felt something sink heavily into my chest, and push against my ribcage with an inordinate force. How do I explain why I have a blinding headache yet again? *It'll get better soon*, they say. Or, *Come over*, they say. *Take a break and have a holiday with us!* I am grateful but cannot accept. I cannot bear to be around the goodness, around the normalcy, around smoothly running homes like the pretty display vignettes at IKEA. Somehow these images invalidate the authenticity of my reality, my existence, my feelings. Every time I return to the cold barrenness of my apartment from the comfort of my friends' kitchens with their giggling children, I am rudely reminded of what I was supposed to have had. It is as if yet again, the invisible collective body at the returns counter smugly declares its judgment: *Leela, you fucked up.*

One of the biggest ghost-pains of suddenly turning into a non-wife is the missing body by my side wherever I go. In the beginning I had assumed that for every place I go and every thing I do, I need another warm body with me. So, I would wait for this friend or that acquaintance to do this or that with me. Somewhere along the way, I got tired of the waiting, tired of the polite enquiries into my well-being when I did have company, and tired of the limitations of togetherness. Recently, I've started going places or doing things by myself, pretending all the while that there's someone next to me with whom I can chat should I need to, and something magical has started to happen. I have begun recognizing myself as a person whose company I've never fully cherished, whom I've taken for granted, whom I've never given a real chance. I have started enjoying this new person so much that sometimes, it is a close call on whether to have company at all! Solo ventures often take me to unexpected places. One, which I had never imagined would have any attraction for me, is the unsightly theater across Lake Washington that plays Bollywood movies. The first time I went there by myself in the middle of the week, it was for a film I really wanted to see, and had grown tired of waiting for others to go with. At the theater I had felt naked, like I had showed up without my dupatta at a puja in Aunty ji's house. I have since discovered the joy of my very own theater row, of indulging in a samosa and chai, and of losing myself in the dreamland of Bollywood: its loudness quieting my inner struggles, its melodrama causing my own drama to pale, its music and color soothing my pain, and somehow, its catharsis allowing me a good purge by the time three hours and ten minutes are up. I usually walk out lighter and happier, tummy full and hands sticky.

I try to re-engage with my reading. Besides the copy of the Seattle Times, I am also holding in my hands M. Scott Peck's *The Road Less Traveled.* In four sections boldly titled *Discipline, Love, Growth and Religion,* and *Grace,* a psychiatrist weaves together a labor of love: his insights from a lifetime spent with people like me, struggling with the various layers of their consciousness and fragments of their pasts. I search for answers between the lines: *Why did he act that way? Why did it happen to me? Why did I allow it to perpetuate?* Guilt shame, and anger intertwine their threads to weave a stifling cloak over my head. Alternately, I feel surges of gratitude; Peck's words, as frequently as on every other page, cause tears to flood my eyes. This book has hidden in its pages and between its lines, my little story. Sometimes the power of being recognized and understood is so overwhelming that I must put the book down and aimlessly skim the vapid newspaper pages.

As I rotate between Peck, the newspaper, and surveying the café, a stark realization begins to dawn on me. I notice that this morning there has been no couple holding hands, no family with two young children, no aging *Princess,* no artist, and no tattooed woman. No, none of the regulars have come by. There is a deathly stillness; there are neither familiar gaits, nor coffee orders. Instead, the Seattle rain appears foreign, and the visitors entering and exiting the café are strangers as well, people I've never seen before, people who aren't here to get coffee. Beyond the intersection, I see a long line of people in tatters, not unlike today's visitors to Elbasha Café, queued up in front of the *Millionair Club.* All of a sudden it hits me. Because today is Thanksgiving all the familiar people – those with *normal* lives – are happily roasting turkey, mashing potatoes or sautéing green beans in their warm kitchens, with familial voices and football commentary afloat in the air. Here, at this intersection, the City of Seattle has retched up all its misfits, those with no warm homes, no roasting turkeys, and no chirpy families. I shudder as another thought occurs to me: here, where I sit, I am more like them than the other café visitors with whom I feel kinship on regular days. Mine is also the vantage point of the vagrant: a vagrant watching other vagrants. For a moment I am horrified.

Then suddenly, I am grateful. Here, with the toothless, inebriated woman and the stumbling man with broken baggage, my existence is vindicated. I am not abnormal, I am not crazy, I am not alone. I am here, with my Palestinian brothers, in the warmth of their café, witnessing the amalgamation of the luxury of coffee and the haplessness of poverty. I see what is real, what is poignant, what is undeniably true. Unlike the peeling layers of my consciousness sheltering me from the full truth, this is all at once in front of me, the harshness of the other end of the spectrum of human existence. I am no longer hovering on the fringe; I am safely in the middle. I have a home, a cover over my head. On the one side I have the homeless of Seattle reminding me that sitting solitarily in a café on Thanksgiving Day is just fine. I have Mahmud and Ghareeb who pamper me with their mother's recipes. I also have my hairdresser Laura, who rubs my scalp with extra care, my banker Tasha, who offers up unsolicited financial help, and my real-estate agent Stephanie, who works overtime to secure me the best deal in a condominium purchase. On the other side I have loving friends and well-wishers offering me the warmth of their kitchens and guest bedrooms, and friends and family calling from distant lands asking after me. I have a brilliant therapist and a gifted massage practitioner, who gently, patiently and lovingly work with me to process my physical and emotional pain. I have Scott Peck, who through a lifetime of loving listening, understands not only *my* pain, but also that of the ghosts of my past, who for reasons of their own, inflicted their pain on me. Most of all, I have the discreet anonymity I need for the healing journey without losing the cushion of a wide support-system that I can access whenever necessary, a quality of American society I had never recognized or appreciated before.

From the perspective of where I sit today, I am able to accept. I accept my pain, my past, my present. And I am grateful for it all, for I learn, and I grow. I have a beating heart, working limbs, a bright mind, and a spirited soul. I have the Almighty watching over me, shining light on my present. On this day of Thanksgiving, from the vantage of my little throne by the piano in Elbasha Café, I gaze out to the rainy streets of Seattle and offer my deep, heartfelt gratitude. *I am here, I am me, and it is all right.*

4

Bearing Mini

Vaishali leaped out of her chair, and practically ran to the bedroom at the end of the hallway. She was positive she had heard little cries, and wanted to make sure Mini wasn't scared, finding herself in the large, unfamiliar bed instead of her American crib. Malini, her sister-in-law, glanced knowingly at her husband. Vivek averted his eyes in a hurry; he didn't want Manish, Vaishali's broad-shouldered Punjabi husband, to notice their exchange. Manish, however, was safely passed out in one of the cane chairs that lined the wall in the living room, his arm dangling, not too far off from toppling a brass oil lamp that stood on the polished terrazzo floor. Four-year-old Rahul ran round and round screaming, "Cousin is here, cousin is here!" and playing pummel horse over the suitcases, which were still strewn across the living room. But the slumbering Manish, awkwardly large compared to his small-framed Andhra in-laws, was also oblivious to the child's rampage. The journey from Houston to Bangalore had been mind-numbingly long and tedious, with serious delays while connecting through Frankfurt. Mini had cried relentlessly on the second flight, stopping only for deep gasps of stale airplane air, and had finally fallen asleep in the car ride from Bangalore International airport, when Vivek had driven them home.

It had been quite the feat to accomplish, to bring the entire family together again. Vivek, the oldest of the three siblings, had worked hard to make it happen. When he had first called his sister about the plans, Vaishali had hesitated to commit to the difficult international journey back to Bangalore, with Mini being just over a year old. But Manish, in his characteristically sensible, no-nonsense way, had reminded her of the importance of being there for this special occasion, and had reassured her that everything would be fine. Even Vishal, the youngest, typically recalcitrant about summons from home, had torn himself away from the demands of graduate school at Columbia to make it back. They had come together to celebrate their father's sixtieth birthday in Vivek and Malini's Ulsoor home, into which, as tradition dictated, the older couple had moved after Dr. Reddy's recent retirement. The plan was to go the full distance and celebrate with traditional Andhra custom; Dr. and Mrs. Reddy, now married thirty eight years, were to have a wedding all over again. Their children were to arrange the ceremony, invite guests and throw a party. Countless arrangements had to be made for the event, which was a mere six days away.

Mrs. Reddy entered the living room with a carved, wooden tray loaded with an array of stainless steel tumblers. "Coffee!" she announced cheerfully, hoping to pump fresh energy into her snoozing son-in-law. The diamonds in her ears had weighed down her lobes, but they sparkled cheerfully, sending tiny rainbows into the surrounds of her pleasant, full face. The matching nose-pin competed for attention. "Where is Vaishali?" she inquired, her tone belying her anxiety, her eyes discreetly searching the room for her daughter. "Oh, she ran into the bedroom," Malini informed her promptly. "She is worried that Mini won't like the new bed," she added. "Ayiyyo, that girl worries too much. Ever since she struggled ..." Mrs. Reddy's voice trailed off. "Vaishu! Vaishu!" she quickly recovered, calling to her daughter like old times. "I have some hot-hot coffee here for you and Manish!" "Coming, Amma!" Vaishali called back, and appeared in the doorway. "Arre, I thought Mini had woken up, but all is fine. The little girl is fast asleep," she said, now smiling to reveal her relief. Manish stirred from his slumber and sat up, happy to see his mother-in-law holding out piping hot coffee, slightly foaming at the top from having been poured out the traditional South Indian way. "Thanks, Amma!" he said politely, and sipped at the bubbles. Seeing him awake Rahul rushed to sit on his uncle's knee, and Manish had to swiftly switch hands to avoid spilling his coffee and burning the little boy. "Calm down Rahul, and sit quietly by me!" Malini scolded her son. "Oh, let him be, he's so excited to have his auntie and uncle and cousin here after such a long time!" Mrs. Reddy gently chided her daughter-in-law in return. Malini rolled her eyes, and Vivek quickly changed the subject. "Are Appa and Vishal still out?" he asked his mother. "You know how the traffic is at this time, they must be stuck somewhere. The temple is quite far away and the priest may have been in the middle of a puja, no?" Mrs. Reddy offered as explanation. Just then they heard the sound of a Bajaj scooter, and Vishal and Dr. Reddy walked into the house moments later. Rahul now sprang from his one uncle's knee to rush to the door, and throw himself at his other uncle with unbridled exuberance. "Mission accomplished!" Vishal announced as he entered the living room. Dr. Reddy followed, and sat down under one of the ceiling fans. The lines in his face were moist with a light sweat, but the delight in his eyes was evident. His three children and two grandchildren were home at the same time.

* * * * *

The early morning noises floated into the bedroom, and stirred Vaishali awake, but the jetlag made her eyelids heavy even two days after arrival. She held on to the covers, reveling in the familiar sounds. Manish, who rarely had much trouble sleeping any where and at any time, was still letting out gentle snores, and in between the two of them, Mini had slept peacefully through the night. Vaishali knew that her mother had already made the morning's coffee, and that her father was probably drinking his second round by now. She could also hear Malini's voice in the kitchen; she was probably making upma or idlis for breakfast. Vishal was likely still asleep like Manish, while Vivek was probably sitting in the living room with their father, drinking coffee and sharing pages from the *Times of India* or the *Deccan Herald*. It comforted Vaishali to mentally complete the picture of her family, listening for the familiar noises and placing everyone neatly in their scripted slots, while still enjoying the privacy of her bedroom. It was something she often struggled to conjure up in their five-bedroom home in Houston, which was palpably silent, empty and lonesome in the morning hours. America just didn't have the Indian household noises; there was neither the maid, nor the series of wallahs who might come by: the milk-wallah, the iron-wallah, the vegetable-wallah, the newspaper-wallah … She thought back to the mornings and nights when Manish had been gone, traveling Monday through Thursday for management-consulting work that took him to client-sites all over the map. In her solitary existence in the house before Mini was born, how she had yearned for the security of the larger familial environment she had grown up with! And she thought of those mornings on which she had stepped into her fuzzy slippers, clutching her belly, hoping against hope … the memory tightened her guts, and she fought to bring herself back to the present.

Later that day, the three women were scheduled to go shopping for silk saris to be worn or given away as gifts at the upcoming wedding ceremony. After lunch they called a taxi, which drove them from Ulsoor to honking, crowded M.G. Road. They walked in and out of several shops filled with sweet incense, sandalwood crafts, and rippling, rich silks, and they finally settled inside *Nalli Silks Arcade* to let the shop-keepers entertain and entice them with hundreds of velvety landscapes. Vaishali had refused to leave Mini behind even with Manish's repeated reassurance that he'd be perfectly happy to look after her, and Rahul had insisted on going along with his baby cousin, even when lured with an afternoon of fun and games with his two uncles. Now he ran around the store, his antics competing for Malini's attention while the shop-keepers unfurled silk after silk with resplendent colors, the intricate borders and various types of booties across the bodies of the saris revealing different regional origins. Vaishali cooed periodically at Mini, who was lying blissfully in her sturdy American pram, which they had struggled to fit into the taxi, which now looked oddly out-of-scale inside the densely packed store. At one point, in a sudden urge to cuddle his cousin, Rahul nearly yanked Mini out of the pram, and Vaishali let out a blood-curling howl that filled the store. The shopkeepers and other shoppers stared, and Rahul began to cry. Malini glared at Vaishali, her voice silent but her angry black eyes communicating shame and fury. Mrs. Reddy quickly ushered Rahul to her side and patted his shoulder, consoling him in a quiet voice. Rahul threw his arms around his grandmother, sobbing and clutching her around the legs. Vaishali took a startled but unhurt Mini in her arms, and murmured sweet nothings into her ear. Malini left the scene, walking outside the store and standing at the street's edge. She breathed in the automobile fumes; the intensity of the late afternoon traffic was oddly soothing to her burning insides.

Eventually, Mrs. Reddy and Vaishali emerged with shopping bags full of the saris they had selected, with Rahul in tow and Mini back in the pram. "Shall we have some coffee and pastries?" Mrs. Reddy tried to inject cheer into the gloom that had befallen the air between her daughter and daughter-in-law. The three women walked back towards Brigade Road, and Vaishali darted into Cauvery Emporium at the corner, for gifts to take back to their few American friends in Houston. She found some sandalwood and bidri artifacts, brass animal figurines, and pearl jewelry for her three closer girlfriends. They walked around the corner and were faced with the colorful, toy-land retail facades of countless shoe, clothing, toy, electronics and music stores. At Vaishali's suggestion, they climbed up to a second-floor Café Coffee Day; she found herself secretly craving their coffee drinks over her mother's quality, home-brewed filter coffee because they were tamer versions of the Starbucks lattes she drank back in Houston. Inside, they ordered a cappuccino each, a couple of chicken puffs to share, and a pastry and soda for Rahul. The energy between the two sisters-in-law was still tense, and Mrs. Reddy good-naturedly did all the ordering, herding the group to sit down and enjoy the afternoon treat.

As they relaxed in the wicker chairs, Vaishali stared out the glass facade to the busy street teeming with shoppers, vehicles and bicyclists. She marveled at how much of the West sat in colorful, glass-metal-and-plastic chunks, playfully and artificially inserted into this old Bangalore street, and yet how different the shopping experience really was in India. She smiled privately at the various teenaged and college-going couples languishing in the couches arranged around the quieter, corner tables. India had been taken over by a café romance, she decided; the coffee shops and shopping malls seemed to be filled with these pseudo-dating couples with nowhere else to go. Vaishali thought back to her own teenage days; she had attended Bishop Cotton's Girls School not too far from where they were sitting just now. It had been relatively close to the Indian Institute of Science, where Mr. Reddy had been a professor, and since they had lived on campus, the radius of her adventures had hardly been expansive. Even in college, she had certainly not frequented any of the snazzy cafés, shopping malls, or five-star bars and discotheques that were popular among young people these days. She had met Manish later, when they were both attending the Indian Institute of Management, and their romance had bloomed in rickety auto-rickshaws, the limited campus grounds, matinee cinemas, or the occasional trip with a group of friends to the Bannerghatta zoo for a picnic on the granite hills.

That evening, as Mrs. Reddy stirred up the sambaar and avial in the kitchen, Vaishali helped Malini set the dinner table. Malini averted her eyes, remaining stiff and aloof even after the men joined in to dine. Mrs. Reddy recounted little stories from their afternoon outing as if it had been nothing short of a merry time, and Rahul joined in, forgetting with a child's abandon, his meltdown in the sari store. "So we are all set then, as far as saris are concerned!" Vivek winked at Manish, and the two men burst out laughing. Vaishali smiled, but Malini remained glum, causing her husband to glance nervously in her direction. "Pass me the bagara baingan, please, Amma?" Vishal asked, oblivious to the tension in the air. Dr. Reddy discreetly scanned the faces of his wife, daughter and daughter-in-law in an attempt to discern what was amiss, but asked or said nothing.

Later, when everyone else was either settled in front of the TV or retiring for the night, Vaishali ran into Malini when stepping out of the bathroom in the hallway. "Malini ..." she started, but Malini turned her face away. "I'm sorry I was upset with Rahul's behavior in the store, but surely you're not still angry about that?" Vaishali persisted, not wanting to let the little incident breed unnecessary ill between them. "I don't know what to say to you, or where to even begin. You're so incredibly selfish!" Malini declared with such scathing scorn that Vaishali recoiled in shock. "What are you saying, Malini?" she asked when she had taken a moment to recover, incredulity filling her voice. "Oh, you're so clueless, aren't you?" Malini was almost yelling now. Luckily, the din in the living room kept the others at bay, and Mrs. Reddy was already in bed. "Are *you* the only mother around here? The only one, I suppose, with her precious, little baby from America! Why do you have to be so bloody protective about Mini? Will a little time with her cousin or uncle or aunt kill her, or what? Can you even see a thing beyond your disinfecting baby wipes and milk formulas and fancy diapers and oversized pram? Is your Mini too delicate for our dirty, third-world India? And is my Rahul any less deserving? Have you forgotten the difficulties with which *he* came into our lives?" Malini didn't stop to breathe; her accusations came hurling at Vaishali in a continuous, overwhelming barrage. Vaishali choked back tears, and she couldn't bring out a word.

She ran into her bedroom and slumped by a sleeping Mini, the tears now streaming down her face. Lying there with her hand on her daughter's belly, Vaishali replayed, as she often did, the vivid memory of Mini's birth. She had hardly been able to believe it when the obstetrician and nurses had handed her the little bundle, after they had pulled the baby out of her numb lower body. Manish, who was normally unflappable, had cried by her side too; they were tears of joy, but also relief from the three years of painful trial they had together endured. Their first fetus, conceived after much trying in the fourth year of their marriage, had terminated in a miscarriage at twelve weeks. The shock and grief had been no less than a death in the family, but Vaishali and Manish had found themselves grappling with their loss in isolation. They hadn't believed that their family or friends would understand; besides, having followed the protocol of keeping their pregnancy confidential until the first trimester was through, it had felt as if they would be reporting the death of a life that had never been. When Manish had returned home from his business trips, he had held her hand late into the night, and Vaishali had cried herself to sleep for weeks on end. The lingering ache in her abdomen had been inexplicable, a sort of dark void and stillness that couldn't be described or measured. It had been a couple of months before she had summoned the courage to tell her mother over the phone; she had never been able to mention anything to Vishal on his occasional calls from New York.

Nearly eight months later, Vaishali had conceived again, and this time they had acted like the pregnancy was a secret even from their own selves, hesitating to mention it much to each other, alluding to it in abstract, distant terms. As Vaishali had crossed off the days on the calendar at work, working through client challenges and tight deadlines, two months had gone by safely, and they had begun to feel some confidence. Then, with the unyielding certainty of Lord Yama's death blow, it had happened once again; the twelfth week had rolled around and Vaishali's uterus had ruthlessly expelled the gently beating life from her body. The blood and mucus had flowed and flowed as blatant proof, but it had been no measure of the enormity of their loss. After the second miscarriage, Vaishali had taken a leave of absence from work and returned to India to recover with her family. Over two months several pujas and temple visits had been undertaken for her health and fertility. It was another ten months after her return to Houston that Mini had been conceived. This time they had simply watched and waited for the inevitable, treating the pregnancy like a terminal illness with a preordained ending. When the twelfth week had come and gone without incident, they hadn't been sure whether to feel relief or greater alarm. It had felt like someone might be playing a cruel joke, waiting for them to fully invest in the life that was taking form before snatching it away once again. But nothing untoward had happened. Vaishali's belly had grown at a normal pace, and under the close scrutiny of her doctors at Texas Children's Hospital, she had carried the baby to full term and given birth with a C-section. Manish and Vaishali had stared at their daughter's lovely, fish-shaped black eyes with utter amazement, and named her Meenakshi.

Due to the uncertainty around Mini's birth, they had not encouraged the common practice of having one of their mothers visit during childbirth, to first participate in the spiraling anticipation of the due-date, and then help the new mother with the abrupt transition from pregnancy and labor, into motherhood. More typically, it was the wife's mother who traversed the many miles to give her daughter support and care, but Mrs. Reddy's wishes to do the same for her daughter had not been fulfilled. Vaishali and Manish had been reluctant to include anybody else in their roller-coaster ride to parenthood, afraid of risking others' heartbreak in the process, and feeling too vulnerable to expose their own fear and distress. So, suddenly, they had found themselves all alone in their brand new adventure, newborn in arms, still feeling wary and tentative, with none of the comfort and cushioning that Vaishali could have accessed from her traditional, close-knit family under other circumstances. Vaishali thought back to the days and nights Manish had been on the road again, when she hadn't had a chance to take a shower all day, let alone glance in the mirror. She had alternated Mini's little mouth between her breasts, changed her diapers every few hours, put her down for a nap that seemed to last only minutes; by the time Vaishali had managed a quick bite to eat, it had been time to run the routine all over again. Her joy had been clouded by a zillion moments of anxiety … every time Mini hadn't latched on to nurse, or had thrown up her feed, or cried endlessly for no discernable reason, or spiked a sudden fever, or had a bad tummy. For every little thing that might be of moderate concern to other fledgling parents, Vaishali had been plagued by a profound, crippling fear of loss, still vulnerable to the fragility of life, as if she were about to awake from a dream and discover that she had no child after all. It had taken Mini's first birthday only a few weeks ago to bolster Vaishali's courage, to finally make her believe that she was indeed mother to a precious little girl. With every gurgle and every giggle from Mini, she prayed, and thanked God for her priceless gift. And when the plan to visit India had materialized, Vaishali's gratitude had been augmented by excitement for little Mini to finally meet her grandparents, uncles, aunt, and cousin. She had been ready and eager to emerge from their prolonged isolation, and become rejoined with the larger, protective envelope she had known so intimately and relied upon all her life. But Malini's words today had put a spear through her heart. With her ear pressed against Mini's back Vaishali drifted from tears to sleep, soothed by the rhythm of her daughter's heartbeat, and was only faintly aware of Manish coming to bed around midnight.

* * * * *

The days were flying by in preparation for the big event. The house was being decorated with elaborate kolam on the floor at the entries and at the center of the living room, strings of bright-green mango leaves framing the doorways, incense burning everywhere, and silver platters of vibuti and kumkum sitting in various places. The house guests were beginning to arrive; some of Dr. and Mrs. Reddy's closest relatives were going to stay with them. The four-bedroom flat was going to fill up quickly, but everyone welcomed the hubbub. Vishal set up a folding metal cot in his parents' bedroom like old times, making one room available to guests, and the long living room wall was lined with rented mattresses for the remaining folks. Through all the preparations Malini kept an unwavering distance from Vaishali, and when they had to complete responsibilities together she remained sullen, talking in terse monosyllables. Vaishali began to notice that her older brother Vivek, her childhood hero, was also being somewhat curt with her. He seemed to be bantering normally with Manish, but he didn't play with or cuddle Mini like he had when they had first arrived. Little Rahul was still his rambunctious self, running about and forever delighted with Mini, but it was evident that Malini was trying to keep her son's enthusiasm in check. Mrs. Reddy was conscious of the inhibited interactions between Malini and Vaishali, but kept whatever feelings she might have, hidden under the armor of pleasantries with their house-guests. She had to visit with her own younger sister and husband, Mr. Reddy's brother and wife, and their two sons and young wives; she couldn't possibly oversee her grown children's struggles. Vaishali, who was accustomed to relying on her mother's explicit and unconditional attention, felt unbearably let down. She managed a few teary words with Manish at night when they snatched brief moments of privacy, and he simply patted her shoulder with his characteristic even-temperedness. "Let it go, sweetheart. You realize that Malini too struggled before they adopted Rahul," he whispered over Mini's sleeping body, reminding Vaishali of a fact that seldom stuck in her mind. She simply loved Rahul as her nephew, placing no attention on the absence of blood ties with the family. She wondered now if she had remained so buried in her own travails, that she had been blind to the experience her brother and sister-in-law had undergone. "Focus on your parents' wedding. This trip is for them; it's why we came all the way despite your trepidation about traveling with Mini," Manish added. Vaishali regarded her husband with gratitude and affection. She reflected with some guilt, that they were spending merely three days towards the end of this trip with his family in Delhi, a significant shortchange to the equal lengths of time they typically tried to devote to each of their families on visits to India.

On the morning of the ceremony, which was to take place around two o'clock in the nearby community center, Vaishali discovered her two brothers and Malini speaking in whispers in the living room. She overheard mention of a Krishtie Antique Art gallery, and couldn't imagine what the huddle was about. When she walked in on them, they stiffened and became visibly uncomfortable. Puzzled and confused, she demanded, "What's going on?" "Oh …" Vivek faltered, and an awkward stillness filled the room. "We were just discussing how to pick up the surprise we've ordered for Amma and Appa," he finally said. "It's a rather large antique carving, and we couldn't hide it anywhere in the flat. So, Vishal is going to pick it up from the gallery in a few hours." Vaishali took it all in, the implications slowly dawning on her. "So you guys are doing a joint present for Amma and Appa?" "Yes ... we were going to ask you if you'd like to join in, but you've been so preoccupied with Mini's sniffles ..." Vivek said flatly. Malini looked away, but Vishal gazed in his older sister's direction with disconcerted, conflicted eyes. "Preoccupied with Mini's cold?" Vaishali said angrily. "She's my child, Vivek! I'm just attending to her needs, for God's sake! You could've just asked me anytime! How could you leave me out of a present for Amma and Appa?" "Well, you could have initiated some ideas too, Vaishali. But it's like you're not even here anymore!" Vivek accused in return. As children, they had religiously planned little surprises on their parents' wedding anniversaries or birthdays, individually taking turns to hatch a plot, with little Vishal following his Akka's or Anna's directions. "Akka, you're welcome to pitch in now. It's not that we want to leave you out," Vishal spoke up for the first time. Vaishali's eyes had begun to sting, and Vishal's words unleashed the floodgates. She stood crying silently for a few moments, before turning back towards her bedroom. As she walked in, she suddenly found her mother behind her. In an unerring, unfailing way Mrs. Reddy had always smelled out her daughter's crises during all those years of growing up, and as an immense consolation to Vaishali, here she was again. "Amma!" she said plaintively, sitting down on the bed and burying her face in her mother's waist like Rahul had done at the sari store. "What is happening, Amma? What do I do now?" Vaishali looked up beseechingly, and found her mother's eyes red and wet, echoing her distress, but with grace and acceptance. "We're no longer one big family, Vaishu. You're becoming different families, separate units," she said slowly, deliberately, sadly.

That afternoon two hundred people gathered in their best silks, the women in their saris and the men in their veshtis, to attend the wedding ceremony of Dr. and Mrs. Reddy. Full-grown plantain trees framed the gates to the hall, fresh and grand kolams adorned the floors, marigolds lit up the space in their flaming splendor, and the notes of the Nadaswaram filled the air with a deeply nostalgic quality. Vaishali watched her parents standing face-to-face, thick rose-and-tuberose garlands in hand, the gray at their temples framing the faces that appeared eternally young to her, and she was moved with a deep urgency. The ties she felt to her family had always been the foundation of her life, the source of her strength, security, and sense of self. And yet, something had irreversibly broken; nothing was ever going to be the same. She shifted her gaze towards her brothers, her two soldiers, across the fire that was sanctifying her parents' union all over again. Their faces blurred as the fumes rose higher, clouding the air between her and them. Off to another side Manish stood holding Mini, and now Vaishali turned to look at her husband and daughter.

Later that night, Vaishali suggested to Manish that they leave the next day – five days ahead of schedule – for Manish's parents' home in Delhi. "Are you sure?" Manish's tone expressed sheer disbelief; it was usually quite the battle to tear Vaishali away from her parents and brothers. Besides, everything had been planned for the whole family to take an overnight trip together, to the ancient stone temples in Belur and Halebid. "Yes," she said with a quiet certainty, and would say no more. The next morning Manish called the Jet Airways office and changed their flights to Delhi for the same afternoon. Dr. and Mrs. Reddy looked surprised by the news of their expedited departure, but neither of them raised any questions or objections. The house was still brimming with guests, and it was in this milieu that they said their premature goodbyes. Vivek offered to drive them to the airport as usual, but Vaishali was firm.

"It's alright Anna, we will be fine. Please just call us a taxi." "Why are they going back already, Baamma?" Rahul demanded of his grandmother, crying and wriggling in her grasp. The taxi pulled away, and Vaishali saw the picture of her waving family at the gates of the apartment complex recede and gradually fade into the dusty wake of the cab, a lingering image of her parents in fine silks with garlands in-hand, supplanting it instead.

As the taxi wound through busy streets towards the domestic airport, Vaishali watched her dreams to move back to Bangalore with her husband and daughter and live near her family, fall away and dissipate like the light rain that scattered on the taxi's windows. They had discussed making an investment in the Prestige Group's upcoming Kensington Gardens project … Manish could consult with the many multinational firms setting roots in Bangalore … Mini could enjoy growing up with her grandparents around, and receive a culturally relevant schooling that Vaishali so dearly valued from her own upbringing … and Vaishali herself could find a meaningful job once Mini was in school … All at once, these long-rehearsed images fizzled out like obliterated sandcastles by the sea. All she could see now in her mind's eye was their Houston home, vacuous but earnest, clinical but functional, lonesome but dependable. She thought of their nice neighbors, their few American friends from her old workplace and Manish's consulting firm, and the vast community of Indians scattered in Houston's suburbs. Vaishali determined that she would return to America, and somehow, weave together a family and a home from the disparate strands within her reach.

5

Kamalamma's Coming of Age

It was four-thirty in the morning on a Sunday. Everyone else in the house was fast asleep, but Kamalamma felt like she had been awake most of the night. Her thin, white, woven cotton sari clung damply to her belly and left shoulder, and her back hurt more than usual. She rose painfully from the low, hardwood bed, and with her bare feet, groped the cold floor for her rubber slippers. Slowly she shuffled to the bathroom, and splashed cold water on her face to take some of the heat off her body. She returned to her chair by the window, and slipped on her reading glasses. She held the four slim prayer books that always sat on the nightstand, and with her leathery hands, rubbed their cheap, plastic covers. Kamalamma was pleased that the shiny pictures of her beloved Gods and Goddesses were protected; Chitra, *God bless her soul*, had done a good job of covering the books with the plastic scraps Kamalamma had been saving for some time. She started to chant from the books, gently swaying back and forth with the rhythm. She was praying, in particular, for her eldest son's recovery from a failing heart and her youngest son's recovery from a failing marriage. But she was also praying for everyone else: her two other sons, her only daughter, her grandchildren, their spouses, and their children.

Kamalamma was a blessed Hindu woman; she had borne four good sons, a rare feat, possible only due to the karma of a previous birth. Since her husband's death in 1996 she rotated through her four sons' homes, spending an equal portion of the year with each of their families. She was like the seasons; like spring, summer, autumn or winter, Kamalamma had appeared at each doorstep for the last five years. Unlike a chirpy spring or a pleasant autumn, however, Kamalamma was rarely welcome. It was as if the privileges earned from her good karma were synonymous with punishment for bad karma that her offspring and their families had somehow incurred.

Despite her progressively stooping back, impaired hearing, and severe diabetes, Kamalamma didn't feel her eighty years in the least. Her sharp, sparkling, roving eyes devoured every detail of the psychedelic world; she hated missing a single moment of action. Frequently her hearing shrugged off its impairment and strained beyond capacity, taking in every whisper uttered. Her tongue was both scathing and witty. Her painful shuffle was easily transformed into brisk motion when called for. Her diabetes frequently took a backseat to anything sweet. And every so often, her deep sonorous voice broke into melodious song, resplendent with the artistry of a young vocalist. Kamalamma did not know how to feel at eighty; she still felt sixteen.

At sixteen, Kamalamma had barely left her childhood. She had sung beautifully and without inhibition, waiting only for half a listening ear before diving into her renderings. She had played the violin. She had jumped and played and pranced around in her colored cotton sari, oblivious of the incongruence of her behavior with her adult dress. "Kamala!" her father had reprimanded, "Behave like the young woman that you are now! Don't you want a respectable groom?" "Grow up, Kamala," her sister, two years younger, had also scolded. "No woman who behaves like that will have her husband attracted to her!" "Chhi, chhi, chhi!" Kamalamma had screamed, clamming her delicate ears shut with her small palms, "Don't talk of impure things to me!" All the house-servants had regularly shielded young Kamala from any housework that her mother assigned to her. "Here, Baby Kamala, we've washed your saris and ironed them for you. No one will know!" One day her father had announced that a young man with a promising future in the government was coming to see her, along with his family. Kamala had been deftly packaged in a silk sari and gold jewelry, puffs of talc to smooth out her face, and a bottu on her forehead. She had been told to sit still and to hide her right hand so they wouldn't notice the missing ring finger. She had sung devotedly within moments of being asked to display her talent. They had been suitably impressed, and few weeks later teenaged Kamala had been married.

The world slowly woke around her as Kamalamma's dutiful chanting climaxed in its intensity. Gradually the day's bustle began, and soon it was time to check if her daughter-in-law was handling the household chores appropriately. She had concluded that Meena, her second son's wife, was the most tolerable of the lot. She was the only one who didn't challenge with snappy, impudent retorts, Kamalamma's karmic right as a mother-in-law to constantly instruct and criticize. Mostly, they were all worthless, kinks in her sons' shining armors, blemishes in gems, thorns in rose bushes. Kamalamma shuffled to the kitchen to get her morning coffee. It had to be enhanced with just the right amount of the artificial sweetener her doctor had prescribed to manage her diabetes. She could tell when four drops had been added instead of three – oh, her conniving, conspiring daughters-in-law! She knew that they purposely squeezed the little plastic bottle harder than necessary. How many times had she instructed them to add three drops of sweetener *without* squeezing the bottle? Kamalamma poured out her coffee with a deftness that belied her eighty years, and carried it to the small round table by the verandah, at which she sat sipping the foam and eyeing the rest of the household as they went about their morning chores. Chitra and Sanjeev were not yet awake; yes, yes, the young couple visiting home from America needed to sleep late into the morning. And then again, Sanjeev was special; he was the first grandson among her grandchildren. He was the name-carrier of Kamalamma's married lineage, and was supposed to plant the seed to propagate it. His wife Chitra was the blessed one to bear the special fruit. Kamalamma's eyes gleamed with anticipation. On such a momentous occasion, tradition dictated that she present the baby male heir with a cup made of solid gold. With this rite, she would earn the highest in karma; in fact, she may even attain moksha!

Kamalamma's first child had also been a boy. Her firstborn, her priceless jewel, had been the product of the terrifying lovemaking of her newly acquired husband. Kamalamma had been shocked and shamed by her husband's advances on the night of their nuptials. How indecent was this man! Didn't he know that women who complied with such behavior were dirty prostitutes, going straight to hell? Kamalamma's husband had patiently waited to educate her; he had brought home a copy of the *Kamasutra,* and had asked her to read it. But poor Kamalamma had only been further aghast and confused. She couldn't understand why no one had told her that the duties of a wife included engaging in ungainly nighttime behavior, and night after night of it at that! But gradually, Kamalamma had become accustomed to it. By the time her second child was conceived, she had even begun to enjoy it and look forward to it.

It was now time for breakfast. Kamalamma heaved herself off her perch, and shuffled over to the dining table. Meena had made idlis, and they didn't look so bad. Before beginning her meal, in a rite of purification Kamalamma expertly swiped her right hand across a brimming steel tumbler, catching a few drops of water to sprinkle them over her plate. Slowly and deliberately she munched her food, watching as everyone else joined in. Ah, Chitra and Sanjeev had woken up in time for breakfast. Now she could regale them with more tales of her yesteryears. Chitra – young, friendly and curious – always made easy prey.

Kamalamma never stopped recounting the grand old days. After all, she had been the wife of a highly-placed, honest and upright officer of the government. Her husband had served during the British Raj, and later in independent India he had chaired an important portfolio. They hadn't been aristocratic, but certainly not poor either! She had played hostess to the grandest of parties. How did it matter that she had had no education beyond middle-school? Kamalamma had an opinion about everything, from how the government should be run, to the details of the cook's daughter's marriage. She had managed the servants well, and had conjured up brilliant menus. She had dressed in bright silks and high heels, and had never missed spraying on a flowery fragrance. Her husband had been the light of every party; with an innate ability to engage the men with intellectual dialogue and charm the women with gentle flirtation, he had never been out of style. Once, when Mr. Patil's wife had declined to attend their party due to a bad headache, Kamalamma's husband had driven over to the Patils' house on his scooter. He had returned a half-hour later with a brightly-dressed and flower-adorned Mrs. Patil perched sideways behind him, her plump right arm jingling with gold bangles and resting gently on his thigh. Kamalamma had burned inside. Over time, in spite of being wildly jealous, she had learned to be secretly proud of her husband's ability to woo other women. After all, she had borne him four sons. She had felt safe.

Once in a while, relatives from her husband's village would show up at their Bombay home, and stay on in search of a better fortune. Among them was her husband's cousin, who had arrived without much notice; he had needed a place to stay to attend college in the city. He was going to be a lawyer. At first Kamalamma had not been happy; there was yet another mouth to feed! Gradually, however, Hariprasad had become Kamalamma's silent confidante and aide. He would occasionally cut vegetables for her, or retrieve heavy pans off high shelves in the kitchen. He would return home early from college, and join her for afternoon coffee with a snack. He would sit quietly on the sparkling floor, and listen to her sing. One day he had told her that she had elegant ankles, just like a dancer's. That night Kamalamma had asked her husband if her ankles were attractive, just as Hariprasad had said. The next morning Hariprasad had disappeared. He had found a cheap place to rent much closer to his college, her husband had explained.

Everyone had left the breakfast table except Chitra. She listened on, transfixed by Kamalamma's gripping narratives. Then rather abruptly Kamalamma was annoyed. Why was Chitra still around, wasting Kamalamma's valuable time, prodding her for stories? She had better, more important things to do! She had some good, socially motivated television soaps to watch, a few clothes to mend, and then she needed to draft two very important letters to powerful people in the government. She was irate; she wanted to give them a piece of her mind regarding the current political situation. Such a state of corrupt anarchy would have never occurred in the government of her husband's time! Oh, those were people of integrity: honest, upright, regally and rightfully powerful leaders of a newly born nation. Kamalamma felt certain she could teach the new generation of inexperienced, corrupt politicians a thing or two. She returned to her room and sat down at the desk with a writing pad and an old fountain pen, her countenance grim and determined. On the upper right corner of the thin, cheap paper it said: Mrs. M. Kamalamma, Social Worker, Wife of Late Mr. M.C. Krishnacharya, Chairman, Transportation Ministry (1950).

Soon, it was lunchtime. Kamalamma shuffled again to the front of the house; she was hungry. She wondered what stale food her daughter-in-law was going to serve up this time. In the days that Kamalamma had run a kitchen, there had never been any leftovers. Food had been prepared daily in plenty in case guests showed up, but always the servants had been given whatever remained at the end of the day. Refrigeration was most certainly an overrated technical invention. Who wanted to consume food that was a whole day old? No economically solvent, self-respecting Brahmin would feel the need to do so. But how was Kamalamma to impress these values upon this generation of women plagued with modernity, splitting their time half-heartedly between unsupervised kitchens and unnecessary careers? Her unfortunate sons were being slow-poisoned daily by their misguided, stubborn, apathetic wives, and Kamalamma could do nothing but be a helpless witness. She muttered under her breath as she sat down at the table. She ate slowly and purposefully, scrutinizing the contents of the others' plates.

Later in the hot, summer afternoon the household slept a silent snooze. Kamalamma sat by herself at the round table near the verandah once again, this time with a stack of playing cards. She laid them out neatly on the table in seven columns, and stared long and hard at them. One by one she turned the various cards, and occasionally let out a triumphant giggle. After four games of Patience were all valorously won, Kamalamma spontaneously burst into melodious song. She closed her eyes, tipped back her head, and sang with devotion and abandon. Through her closed eyes she could see her music teacher, the gawky man who used to come to the house every other morning when her husband had the post in Bombay. On the days of her lessons Kamalamma had bathed with extra care and worn flowers in her hair. She had wrapped up her kitchen activities early and waited impatiently for her teacher to arrive. His face, with the three white marks of vibhuti streaking his forehead and pencil-thin mustache lining his upper lip, was vivid in her memory. He had sung to her and she had followed, and the mellifluous union of their voices had been unparalleled. One day a neighbor had enquired of Kamalamma's husband, about the man who visited his wife every other morning. The next day her husband had politely told the music teacher that Kamalamma was too busy running a teeming household to spare any time for music lessons. That, Kamalamma knew for sure, was the turning point in the unmaking of a brilliant vocalist.

After three elaborate compositions were generously offered to an imaginary audience, Kamalamma stirred from her reverie. She shuffled across the room and into the kitchen, popping a handful of milky sweetmeats into her mouth from a plastic container hidden deep inside the refrigerator. As she moved through the corridor towards the back of the house, she overheard muffled, rhythmic sounds from behind Sanjeev and Chitra's bedroom door. Kamalamma paused outside, tightened her hearing aid, and stood motionless for a while. Then she continued on towards the verandah, and opened the wooden door leading outside. She reached painfully for the clothesline, and undid the wooden clothespins that held the garments hung to dry earlier in the day. Back inside the house, she carried the clothes into her room and laid them out on her bed. Slowly, but with surprisingly steady hands, Kamalamma began folding everything into neat piles. She inspected each garment as she did so: everyone's towels, a silk blouse belonging to her daughter-in-law, a familiar shirt of her son's, her own cotton petticoat. Then there was this unfamiliar piece of satiny material. It looked expensive; it must belong to

Chitra. Kamalamma turned the silky, black undergarment around in her weathered hands and rubbed it repeatedly, fascinated by its soft feel. With two of the three fingers on her right hand, she traced every seam, the straps, and the wire underneath the cups. Then she held it against her small chest, and stared in the mirror.

Kamalamma slumped on her bed next to the pile of clothes; she felt exhausted all of a sudden. She lay down on her back and closed her eyes, her distended belly protruding into the air, the end of her sari slipping from her frail shoulder. In her stupor Kamalamma was in a small, dark room, sitting on the edge of a large bed whose posts were lined with fragrant tuberoses, as on a night of matrimonial consummation. She was draped in a silk sari, but wore no blouse. All she had on over her bosom was a black, satin bra. Her husband was approaching her slowly, his narrow shoulders hunched awkwardly, and as he moved closer she could see he was naked. He bent towards her and reached to caress her silken breast. "You ... have ... come ... of ... age ..., Kamala," his voice echoed. She could now see his face more clearly in the stream of moonlight through the window; it had a pencil-thin mustache lining the upper lip and three white lines of vibhuti streaking the forehead. Kamalamma screamed. She awoke sweating and shaking. The neatly folded clothes had tumbled to the floor, and all the garments lay scattered. Kamalamma clutched the end of her sari and wiped her perspiring forehead. She groped frantically for her slippers, and grabbed the four plastic-sheathed books from her nightstand. She swayed fervently with loud and frenzied chanting, pressing the prayer books tightly to her chest.

"Amma! Amma!" Are you alright?" Chitra ran into the room and laid her palm across Kamalamma's clammy forehead. "Would you like your evening coffee now, Amma?" Kamalamma's eyes were still distant. Then suddenly she rose from her seat, almost businesslike. She straightened and patted down her sari, combed her thin, gray hair into a tight bun, and puffed her face with sweet-smelling sandalwood talc. "Yes, yes, it is time for my coffee. Tell her to add not *one* more than precisely three drops of sweetener."

6

No Parking

I rolled over yet again, grunting, trying to find the position that would make me comfortable. Curling up like a kidney bean seemed to suit me best. The cramps came in waves, in and out, up and down, typical of the darned stomach flu I catch at least once a year. Now I was hot, now I had the shivers; I couldn't keep the covers on, I couldn't keep them off. Outside, the temperature was already 36 degrees Celsius and rising, not uncommon in the peak of Delhi summers. The morning's activities carried on in the background: the maid was washing dishes, the gardener was watering the lawn and flower beds, the milkman had just delivered the liter of milk for the day, and Mummy was rushing around madly as she always did getting ready to leave for work. It sounded like Papa was going to be off running errands too; he was scheduled to leave the next day on one of his international lecture tours to London, Sydney, Johannesburg and God-knows-where-else. Normally I would've been leaving behind the chaos in the house to catch the U-Special teeming with college students going to Delhi University, but extreme dehydration and the need for a proximate toilet had together conspired to keep me homebound and mostly in bed. On one of my runs to the toilet and back, I overhead Papa saying something about having to make a trip to the Standard Chartered Bank in Connaught Place to get travelers checks for his trip, among a zillion other last-minute things he had to accomplish. Mummy was asking him how he was going to get there, since our only car, a ten-year-old, baby-blue Fiat with a sticker on its dashboard that said *Jesus Never Fails*, that all of us secretly considered auspicious, was at the repair shop. Papa mumbled something about the mechanic having promised to have the car ready by the early afternoon. I stumbled back to bed, and a nagging feeling at the back of my head told me that he was, yet again, about to venture off secretly with his little Kinetic Honda scooter. No doubt Mummy wasn't buying his story either. Driving that scooter around the city was illegal for Papa, not just in his wife's terms, but literally, because it was against real law. You see, although Papa had a driver's license for the car, he didn't have one permitting him to drive anything on two wheels!

Reading about other countries that work like clockwork in the developed world, I had come to the conclusion that it was impossible to make sense of most things in India. How the world's largest democracy functions and thrives could be the subject of a never-ending dissertation spanning several lifetimes. Perhaps this is why some Indians are reborn, so that they can make sense of India and how she works, or doesn't, over and over and over again. Moksha, or Nirvana, if you follow Siddhartha's footsteps, is simply unattainable. All I can say is that when you zoom out far, far back to telescopic distances, there may be, just may be, some consistent, organic pattern to it all. Kind of like the fractal structure of a coastline, you know? At the microscopic level, however, nothing makes sense. So, one of the things that just didn't make sense was why Papa had an "automobile" license but not a "motorcycle" license, while I, an eighteen-year-old college-going gal, happily sported a driver's license that permitted me to drive both types of vehicles. Anyway, maybe it had something to do with the roots of Papa's very first Indian driver's license, which could be traced back to our years in the deep south of India in the late seventies. At the time, perhaps the Tamilians, a shrewder lot, were simply not issuing combined licenses just like that. Now, fourteen years later in India's dusty, hot capital, kids were getting their hands on licenses that said "car and motorcycle," but their parents were suddenly required to pass special tests to drive a two-wheeler. And for whatever reason, Papa had been failing the test repeatedly. He claimed it was because what they really wanted was a bribe, and since he wouldn't pay one they would have him do all these ridiculous moves with the scooter, like drive around in formations of the number eight. Then they'd fail him on ludicrous pretexts like he didn't hand-signal when he began turning on the top of the eight, or because he put one foot down at the intersection of the loop in the eight, which is just not kosher for good scooter driving. You might wonder who in real life goes around in eight-formations on their scooter, busy showing both electronic and hand signals at each curve in the formation. But then didn't I say that not much in India makes logical sense? I wasn't complaining though; it felt pretty good to be one up on Papa in driving matters.

"Bye Sonali!" Papa called. "Feel better soon … and do make sure to drink lots of water!" I decided to check on Papa in return, something I had started to do in my later teens. "Papa, you're not driving the Kinetic Honda all the way to Connaught Place are you?" I called back. "Oh, no, no, I don't really take it off campus, just like we agreed!" he said, appearing briefly in my doorway to assuage my fears, and then left the house. Yeah, right. After Papa had repeatedly failed his driving test, he had declared that he was going to keep renewing his learner's permit, and drive the scooter only within the Jawaharlal Nehru University campus, from home to the Department of Language and Linguistics, and back. "That's why I bought the scooter anyway, for the short, daily commute within campus!" he often reassured us, as if things were going just as he had originally planned. But both Mummy and I knew that he'd begun straying outside the boundaries, now to pick up sweets and samosas from *Moonlight* in Munirka, or then to buy fresh fish from *Gujarat Fisheries* in Hauz Khas, and so on. The radius of his ventures was gradually growing, and for some reason, like a child hiding himself in a mound under his blanket, he simply assumed we didn't know. What ever escapes Mummy's watchful eagle-eye anyway?

After Papa left on the scooter, its distinctive sound zooming off into the distance, a spell of silence fell on the house. The pitter-patter of our coffee-and-chocolate cocker spaniel approached me: hop, skip and jump, and soon a warm lump formed by my feet. We were loyal pals, Snuggles and I. Everyone seemed to think that it's really hard to be a single child, but with Snuggles around, I hadn't really felt it in a long time, not after I was about eleven, anyway. I could never forget the day Mummy reverted from her *It's me or a dog* pledge, and brought home a five-week-old silk bundle with trembling legs. It's true, though, we did kind of live disparate, solo lives: Mummy in her work as a research scientist at the All India Institute of Medical Sciences, Papa with his incessant stream of international conferences, book projects and teaching duties, and I ... well, I in my own fantasy world of dreams, wonderings and musings. I often wondered why Mummy and Papa got married, and why they even had me. Ever question why you were born? Why you didn't get to choose ... your birth, or your parents? Or, how about *where* you were born?

I was born in the United States of America, and this was currently posing a great dilemma for me. Mummy and Papa had received their doctorate degrees in America and returned to India when I was two, quite unlike their cohort of Indian graduate students in the late-sixties-and-early-seventies, post-Vietnam America; most Indians at the time never returned home once they had tasted America, you know. And now at eighteen, thanks to my parents' unusual and ideological choice, I was suddenly stuck between two identities. It was time for me to leverage my birthright and choose American citizenship, but since India and America didn't have something called a reciprocity agreement, I needed to give up my Indian citizenship if I chose to be American! I really didn't know what I wanted … I did know I wanted to attend graduate school in America like my parents had, and Papa kept telling me with perfect pragmatism totally at odds with the idealism he was reported to have exuded in his own youth, how everything in my life would be so much easier if I were American. Pragmatism aside, he even tried to instill in his counsel a bigger vision. "By carrying an American passport you can have a global life! You can visit, live and work in so many places in the world. Your reach will be larger and wider." "But how can I be American? I grew up here, in India!" I protested, a mild sting starting in my eyes. I was miserable, hating that I had to choose between two loyalties. Lying in bed with my tummy flu I was muddling through my big dilemma all over again when Snuggles did what he did best; he snuggled up closer, warmer, tighter. I stroked his long, silky ears, he gave me a couple of warm licks, and soon I drifted into a comfortable, worry-free sleep.

* * * * *

There was a loud, urgent thumping on the door. Snuggles had begun barking just moments earlier, and I sat up like a bolt, my legs stiff, thinking that in the last moments of my sleep I'd heard one of those noisy auto-rickshaws pulling up outside. I stumbled to the door in my pajama-clad shambles and said instinctively, "Who is it?" "It's me, Papa, open up quick, beta!" I detected a mix of urgency and despair in his voice. I opened the door to see my father looking not only terribly anxious, but also rather sheepish, and with him, the 42-degree heat swept into the house. Snuggles jumped up and down joyfully, delighted by Papa's unexpected return and oblivious to his worries. "You've *got* to save me! You *must* bail me out!" Papa said dramatically with total haplessness in his eyes, and my tummy twisted in alarm. "What? What in the world happened, Papa?" "Well, you know how I had to go to the Standard Chartered Bank? But the damned mechanic didn't have the Fiat ready as promised; you know these mechanics, they never keep their word! Anyway, with hardly any time left before my travels tomorrow, I thought that just this once I would ride the scooter to Connaught Place … you know, just quickly there and back … all I had to do was park for a few minutes, dart in and out of the building." Papa was breathless in his report, mouthfuls tumbling out with no intermission. "You know how my banker typically has everything prepared in advance … anyway, I went in, finished my work in ten minutes flat and came out; everything had gone fine, and then I found: the scooter was gone! Those bastards, they simply took it away … in the ten short minutes that I was gone, they managed to tow me!" Papa exclaimed, apparently still in disbelief. I didn't know where to begin my interrogation. First, he'd gone and driven that silly thing all the way to Connaught Place, and now it was missing; amazing what fathers of teenagers did these days. "Who's "they," Papa, and why would they take your scooter?" I began. "Oh, I guess I forgot to say," Papa replied with downcast eyes, "I had mistakenly parked it in front of a No Parking sign."

This was unbelievable. Not only had Papa driven the scooter illegally to the heart of New Delhi where the police fine people left and right, he'd even left it in a no-parking zone! What was he thinking? And now he couldn't retrieve it from the pound because he had no valid license, so he wanted me to schlep with him – in my pajamas, dehydrated and with the tummy runs – all the way to bloody Connaught Place in the scorching heat. I huffed and puffed as I changed into jeans and a T-shirt, then grabbed a bottle of water and stepped outside. Snuggles was most disconcerted with the illogical sequence of events; one human returned home but two were leaving in the bargain? The auto-rickshaw driver had waited to take us back – Papa obviously had *this* part figured out – but the ride wasn't pretty. "You're really going to owe me big!" I yelled grumpily over the deafening rickshaw rattle. "Yes, yes, anything you want, sweetheart!" Papa yelled back with whole-hearted compliance. Ah, I could've asked for a new car! We dove in and out of potholes, getting shaken to the bone, and my tummy rumbled in protest, with nothing but water bumping my insides. We made our way through afternoon traffic, in which the heat and dust mixed with automobile exhaust to form a special concoction for our lungs.

It was somewhere around the salmon buildings of Bhikaji Cama Place that we were stalled at one of many traffic lights, with beggars and their naked children poking their browned, skinny arms into our auto rickshaw, when Papa launched into formulating an elaborate strategy for how best to deal with the authorities. "Beta, let's discuss your approach to these guys at the pound. I think you should tell them that *you* went to the bank on your parents' behalf, and that totally mistakenly, not intentionally at all, you parked in the No Parking zone. You just couldn't see the sign, the way it's hidden behind a tree, you see! Oh, and don't forget to tell them that your father is a professor at JNU," he added, his chest swelling with importance. "God, Papa!" I exclaimed, rolling my eyes and throwing back my head with practiced scorn. "You *really* think those bums will give a damn who I am, or who my father is? All they care about is the fine, Papa! And maybe a bribe too, the bribe you so proudly refused to pay the driving-test administrators! And when *are* you going to pop your head outside the big bubble of Indian middle-class ideology and realize that being a professor is not the ultimate status, anyway?" Papa fell silent. I coveted any opportunity to turn my nose up at his educator-is-supreme outlook that smelt oddly like the caste system, and I was making full use of this one being offered to me on a silver platter. Under normal circumstances I would've received an earful about my "teenage cynicism" and a considerable dishing of discipline, but this time the shoe was on the other foot. Ha!

The auto-rickshaw stuttered and sputtered along the broad, tree-lined boulevards and endless traffic roundabouts that make up Edwin Lutyens's Baroque New Delhi, and my mind hopped randomly between the present quest to release the Kinetic Honda on Papa's behalf and my citizenship dilemma. Yes, the first-world was promising, but something about this third-world chaos tugged at my heart. Where else could I see, smell and experience every cross-section of the human condition all at once on a single, broad avenue, like I was doing in this very moment? In a rare coincidence of opinions Mummy agreed with Papa about what my direction should be. My two girlfriends from high school also thought I should turn American; they just thought it would be cool. They laughed about some future day when I might even marry a gora and have mixed-color babies. I resented the frivolity with which they viewed my existential crossroads, but it was hard not to laugh along anyway. My newly-made, first-year college friends at St. Stephens didn't remotely comprehend my dilemma either; what was I fretting about? I had a winning ticket to the American Dream, and I was having feelings of attachment to third-world India? Where was I, stuck in some dated, sentimental, patriotic Bollywood movie of the black-and-white era?

The thoughts racing in my mental maze were arrested when, at long last, we arrived at the repository for impounded vehicles. Our auto-rickshaw driver appeared to know all about vehicle-towing, and he pulled up confidently in front of an old, elegant but dilapidated colonial structure, that looked nothing like a pound. Papa paid him forty rupees and thanked him ceremoniously with a gratuitous thump on his back. We walked through a colonnaded perambulatory for an inner courtyard space, except that the perambulatory wasn't an ordinary surround; quickly it revealed itself to be a penitentiary of sorts for female detainees. As we crossed the threshold into the courtyard following small, inconspicuous signs of floppy cardboard that said "impounded vehicles release office," with red arrows hand-drawn next to the letters, a policewoman dragged a haggard woman by her hair into one of the rooms, mouthing off crass expletives all the while. It all felt surreal, and I shuddered even in the heat. Papa seemed to not even notice; he was too intent on the important interview he presumed we were going to have shortly, in order to retrieve our pathetic little scooter. As we walked across the unexpectedly large courtyard – nearly the size of a sports field – towards the room in which the "release" was supposed to happen, we saw in the distance a happy congregation of two-wheelers, on which even happier goons had propped themselves. They were smoking beedis, cackling impertinently, and hurling profanities at each other. Papa glared from a distance as if this might be sufficient to scare them away, but his efforts dissipated like wisps of smoke in the hot air. The bare ground was radiating high afternoon heat like nobody's business, making my already light head spin round and round. We entered the tiny office, and there he was, the quintessential Delhi-government-clerk: finger up his nose, chewing tobacco, lackey to the side, a table fan blowing hot air, stashes of paper strewn everywhere, and radio blaring in the background. While Papa hovered in the back, nudging me with last-ditch pleas to enact his recommended daughter-of-professor script, the clerk made no eye contact whatsoever with either of us. As soon as I appeared at his desk, he just asked me for the scooter's license-plate number and my driver's license, stated the fine of rupees one-hundred-and-thirty-eight, took my money, made me sign a scrap of flimsy pink paper, and handed me a carbon copy. "Yes, you can take it away now!" he said, not once looking up. It took three minutes in all. Satisfied that everything went so well, we approached the little army of scooters, and shooed off the bums to get access to our silver one. I extended my hand to Papa for the keys, and then it happened again. Papa's face blanked. "What is it now?" I asked. "Err …, I don't know where … Oh no!" "*What* Papa?" It was hot, I was weak, and my patience was running dangerously low. "I left the helmet in the auto-rickshaw!"

Oh fuck. This was it. It was almost 1:30pm, just around the hottest time of Delhi afternoons; we were standing behind a women's penitentiary with a bunch of vagabonds staring at us, we finally had our scooter to go back home, but no helmet. We wouldn't get past the first traffic light with a helmet-less driver; the law, for yet another ridiculous Indian reason, still didn't mandate that the pillion rider have protective headgear, but had serious implications for the driver not wearing a helmet. I stared futilely at Papa for a long time, simply speechless. Then, with a few deep breaths to help my tummy stop protesting, I said as calmly as I could, "Well, Mummy has been asking you to replace that silly, strapless excuse you wear on your head and pass off as a helmet, so I suppose it's just as well that it's gone. Let's go find a shop and buy you a new one." Papa now wore the expression of a child for whom nothing at all was going his way. He shuffled along, disgruntled, and we began walking towards Connaught Place's colossal ring of retail.

Then Papa realized he had no cash on him. We stood in the middle of the street, with honking buses, cars, rickshaws and cyclists, trying to figure out what to do next. Our only choice appeared to be to head back to the Standard Chartered bank with the No-Parking sign, and cash out some of Papa's travelers checks back into rupees, and *then* find a helmet store. I tried to remain supportive in my attitude, but this was mounting into an impossible, endless, infuriating quest. My only respite came from evil machinations of how, in the future, I would leverage the events of this day to my advantage, especially when inundated with Papa's smug, professorial lectures on how I should live my life. By the time we arrived at the wrought iron gates of the bank, it was 1:58pm, and the stick-thin, armed guard at front was just in the process of drawing the accordion-like metal gates together for closing time. Like the just-in-time scene of the most melodramatic Bollywood flick, Papa began running towards the entrance flailing his arms and flinging them between the gates just as they were about to lock in place. You could visualize this scene in slow-motion, an impressive army of violins screaming in the background score. He practically fell to his knees in front of the puny guard, "I *must* go in; it is a matter of life and death!" Bewildered, the guard backed off and let us through. Five minutes later, we emerged with a thousand rupees in cash stashed away in Papa's passport folder, and I began to feel a glimmer of hope that I could crawl in bed again soon.

We traced our way back to the Connaught circus area, and scoured the storefronts for a shop that might stock helmets. People and vehicles were running helter-skelter in the mid-afternoon traffic, and the weak and giddy feelings in my body returned with a vengeance. We stopped to get a soda each, and proceeded, searching here and looking there, spotting everything but a helmet store. Finally, on a hunch, I took us down Vivekananda Road, one of the offshoots just past the road to the New Delhi railway station, and there it was, a store with an array of colorful, round, shiny objects. "Found it!" I screamed in delight, never having felt so happy to see a plethora of helmets. I asked the guy for a top quality one, and turned around to look at Papa, only to find him wearing an expression of backpedaling. I was having none of it; this was my day of upper-hand. "Papa, really, we've had enough drama for one day. Now that you are spending the money, let's get you a really good helmet. It'll make Mummy happy, and you'll be less worried when I drive the scooter around too." I threw in the last bit knowing it would have a desirable effect, and it did. Promptly, Papa fished out the money from his passport folder, and parted with rupees eight-hundred-forty-four. Shiny, silver-blue rotunda in hand, we marched triumphantly up the offshoot back towards Connaught circus. "I'm exhausted Papa; please let's just catch an auto to the pound," I pleaded. "Of course, of course, beta," Papa agreed generously, his spirits having risen considerably at the prospect of finally extricating the scooter and heading home.

We found an auto-rickshaw at Connaught circus and jumped in, but within moments Papa paled yet again. I didn't want to ask. I looked at him blankly, the tiredness now seeping to every extremity with such fervor that I was sure I would pass out. "Oh goodness," he started, with the familiar introduction of the day. "I think I left my passport folder in the helmet shop." Papa's voice was the smallest I'd ever heard it. I began screaming nonsense. The auto-rickshaw driver looked terribly alarmed. "Go around the circle to where you picked us up, and stop there for a few moments, okay?" I yelled at him in sheer madness. He nodded silently, and now we were weaving through the one-way traffic to circle all the way back to where we had started out. Back down the offshoot, into the store Papa and I darted, and by some stroke of heavenly luck, there it was, the black leather folder, sitting untouched on the counter. Papa grabbed it, smiling apologetically at the shop-owner and informing him in Hindi, "Sorry, I left my folder here," and bolted out of the store like he had just stolen something in broad daylight. The shopkeeper looked unfazed, as if nothing extraordinary had happened, and just stared mechanically at our movements through his store. I followed Papa into our waiting auto rickshaw, and we headed back to the pound.

Back we went through the women's penitentiary, across the courtyard, towards the assembly of towed vehicles, and shooed off the vagrants once again. Déjà vu. Papa was assuming the stance of driver, and wordlessly, I extended my hand to him for the keys. There was no way I was having him drive us back, given the fucking farce we had just played all afternoon. He submitted without protest. Besides, I was the licensed driver of the two, wasn't I? But as I weaved my way back towards South Delhi through traffic and around the endless roundabouts, Papa was determined to contribute his learned years to the return journey. At every turn he began to show hand-signals with unparalleled vigor and demonstrativeness. He was practically turning us over with the force he was exerting. "Please stop that, Papa!" I shouted into the hot breeze. "No need to practice your hand-signals now, no one's testing you!" I added cheekily. Finally I was having some fun. The new helmet felt sturdy, the sun was beginning to lower in the sky, my tummy was settling down, and I was getting to drive with Papa propped obediently at the back. Perhaps it hadn't been such a terrible day after all!

As we pulled up in front of our campus quarters, we found the mechanic waiting there with the Fiat. His assistant had followed him on a scooter to give the boss a ride back to the shop. "Completely fixed, Sir ji!" he said, puffing his chest like a proud peacock upon seeing Papa. "You never have anything done in time, Manjit Singh ji!" Papa gave the mechanic the customary berating, which Mr. Singh dutifully accepted with a fake apology-laugh. Then Papa went inside the house for cash to pay off Manjit Singh. Mummy wasn't home yet. She usually took the bus back to the JNU campus from her institute, and the timings of the Ring Road-circling 666 line were erratic enough to make her return unpredictable within an hour's range. I liked to call the bus-route the Devil's Loop. "Quick, get back in your pajamas!" Papa ordered, implicitly proposing a pact to keep the day's events a secret between us. While I obliged him by going into my bedroom to change, he walked into the living room, poured himself a stiff scotch, and collapsed on the couch. Snuggles was beside himself, running back and forth in a mad loop between the rooms to alternately get petted by the two of us. I fixed myself a lassi, and followed a galloping Snuggles into the living room. There, I found Papa all stretched out, head thrown back and drink balanced on his knee, and I began to laugh out loud. He broke into a bellowing laugh too, and Snuggles became even more animated, excited to participate in whatever was so funny.

"So, you really think Mummy won't know?" I asked Papa, making myself comfortable in one of the chairs, with *The Fountainhead* in my lap. "How could she?" he grinned. Everything is just as it was, isn't it? The Fiat is back, I have my travelers checks..." "Yes ... *and* a spanking new helmet!" I reminded him. "Oh, hmmnn," he mused for a moment. "Well, I'll just tell Mummy that I finally decided to take her advice and buy myself a proper helmet. That should make her happy!" Papa's grin widened and his expression turned triumphant, even smug, as if this entire thing had been his plot to begin with. I rolled my eyes and turned to Ayn Rand, hoping that Howard Roark's uncompromising ethic might shed some light on my life's present dilemmas.

* * * * *

Mummy returned home from work at about six in the evening. Snuggles began his jumping routine again, delighted to have the last member of the family back in the house. I held my breath for the inevitable question ... and there it was. Mummy had barely taken off her heels when she asked from the entryway, "Where did this new helmet come from?" From behind the pages of my book, I held my breath. Papa looked up and said with convincing innocence, "Oh, since I went all the way to Connaught Place, I thought I should look into getting a new helmet." "You've been asking me to get one for so long!" he threw in, feigning gratitude for her concern. "Well, where's the old one?" Mummy retorted quickly in his heels, wasting no time in being impressed. "Err..., the old one...?" Papa stammered, not having foreseen this one. "Why do

I need the old one?" "Well, they might soon require the pillion riders to wear one, right?" Mummy said, now walking into the living room, looking just as prim and spiffy in her tightly wrapped, printed chiffon sari as she had looked leaving the house several hours ago. "Ah, yes, but you never like riding with me, do you? And if you ever change your mind, we can always get another good helmet, right? Why bother keeping around an old, useless one?" I kept my face unwaveringly covered with my novel, afraid I might burst out laughing if I caught either Papa's or Mummy's eye. "How are you feeling, Sonali?" Mummy gave up and switched topics, much to Papa's relief. "Oh, I'm much better now, Mummy!" I replied. "Did you drink a lot of water and lassi through the day, and get enough rest?" she persisted. "Oh yes, Mummy!" I assured her, images of auto rickshaws, beggars at traffic lights, thugs on scooters, helmets in a store, armed bank guards and hair-dragged female prisoners flying rapidly through my mindscape like a spectacular Bollywood flashback.

"I had such a long day, and the bus just wouldn't show up. I had to wait thirty-five long minutes at the bus stop!" Mummy was just launching into her usual 666 rant, when I heard the all-too-familiar sputter of an auto rickshaw. I thought I might be imagining it, having spent most of my afternoon in one of those bone-rattling things, but moments later there was a loud rapping on the door. "Who could it be at this time?" Mummy pondered out loud, frowning. Papa leaped out of his comfy perch, nearly spilling his whisky on Mummy's coveted, six-hundred-and-fifty-knots-per-square-inch, silk-on-silk Kashmiri rug. He rushed to the door, clearly hoping to wrap matters up quickly, but Mummy followed close behind. Snuggles was barking his head off. Outside, a man stood in the falling light, holding in his hands a gray, beaten-up round thing with ratty, dangling straps. "Your helmet was left behind in my auto rickshaw, sahib! So I drove back all the way after my afternoon rounds to return it to you!" It was our loyal, conscientious auto rickshaw driver who had driven us to the pound!

Mummy's eyes narrowed into her characteristic, piercing glare, and her face had burning questions written all over it. Papa's was ashen. I hid mine safely behind Ayn Rand's masterpiece, but began to let out tiny giggles.

7

Someday

They lay together on the carpeted floor in the bare room upstairs, her ear pressed tightly to his chest, straining to record every heartbeat through the soft folds of his cotton T-shirt. His right arm cradled her lightly, and when she hummed she could hear the tune reverberate through his ribcage and back into her own head. It was as if her melody traveled to his soul and returned to her faithfully, augmented by the rhythm of his heartbeat and the spark of his spirit. Her slender fingers stroked his blonde-brown hair, and then traced the arch of his eyebrows to the bridge of his nose, pausing there briefly to harness the energy from his mind before returning to the beginning of the cycle. His fingers returned the affection, unmindfully running straight lines down her arm, making imaginary furrows. *How white his fingers are against my brown skin*, she thought.

Maya was seeing David after what felt like eons. Granted, she had seen him last week, but that had been after months. After all, they used to see each other every day over lunch or coffee, sometimes dinner, and talk on the phone on most nights. Their conversations verged on eternal exchanges, roaming the earth and scanning every subject under the sun, like perpetual motion in a frictionless atmosphere. Topics sprung everywhere like baby-green shoots in a rapidly proliferating vine, and parentheses opened branch-stories to augment the parent thread, but David and Maya never lost their way in the boundless space they navigated together. The vivid, animated repartee only paused when sleep began to slur David's speech. Sleep was the friction: it consumed him like hypoglycemia, he said. But the thread could be seamlessly picked up at the next available opportunity, like there had been no time in between. Subjects for conversation never ran out, nor were stories ever exhausted in the collective repository. If they were repeated, there was always the newfound, delightful nuance to be elucidated, or the special highlights to be exclaimed in unison to produce greater amazement, renewed disgust, or fresh peals of laughter. And then there had been the deathly silence. After several months Maya had slowly and painfully resurfaced, like a crushed seedling re-rooting itself and extending its frail limbs to the sun once again. Six days ago, she had chosen to appear at the door to David's new hideout: a three-bedroom house in a gritty Seattle neighborhood. And she had come to see him again today.

Barely an hour earlier Maya was a guest in a birthday party for a one-year-old. Thirty minutes into arriving at the party, she had begun to feel slightly nauseated. Thirty adults and a handful of kids had been squatting in folding chairs in a backyard of blissful, suburban America, circled around a never-ending pile of presents, cooing and clapping as each mound of paper was unwrapped to reveal one more brightly-colored, plastic contraption destined for the landfill. The little girl had been busy attacking the dirt in a small herb-patch in the yard. Her father had scooped her up in his arms every now and again, dangling in front of her yet another prize for making the one-year milestone on the planet, but the child had repeatedly slithered out of his grasp to reach for the dirt again. And so the afternoon had ensued. Time had ticked away in Maya's head like a timed bomb. *Tick, tick, tick.* If one didn't wish to delve enthusiastically into the gift display, one had the option of taking another helping from a large pile of hot dogs, or from an oversized, frosting-laden cake. After levitating above the vapid proceedings for a while, Maya had felt a welling urge to punch someone or scream her lungs out. Instead she had said crisp, polite goodbyes and jumped in her car, bursting into tears as she sped onto State Route 99. The feeling of being totally on the fringe, of identifying with no one and nothing at the gathering, had engulfed her. Through blurry vision she had continued speeding southwards, past her apartment building, past downtown and along the waterfront towards an unknown escape. It wasn't until the edge of the port of Seattle had emerged in the horizon – with the large, regular shipping containers, the bright orange cranes, and the seemingly immobile gray-black barges – that she had felt her suffocation release. Then, acting in characteristic impetuousness she had pulled off the exit to David's house and knocked on his door. *Only David would know.*

Standing at the brick-red door Maya felt like a twelve-year-old at the base of her best friend's secret tree-house in the forest. David's head emerged tentatively on the third round of rapping, by which time Maya had turned around to leave. As always, his tousled hair and wide-eyed expression reinforced the eternal boyishness that hung about him. Mild confusion and sheepishness gave way to surprise and delight, crossing his face in mixed shadows before he said eagerly, "Come on in, I'm drawing!" It had been just like that last week as well. No matter how much time had elapsed or what unmentionables had occurred in between, David greeted

Maya as if he had seen her only yesterday and everything was still the same. *Why was she hesitating then?* He looked a trifle puzzled. Maya followed him up the stairs into his barely furnished office, and collapsed in a heap on the carpeted floor. "I'm a misfit in this world!" she proclaimed, throwing off her sunshades, nearly in tears again. David settled quietly on the floor next to her, neither making any overt gestures to console her, nor undertaking any explicit enquiries. He simply maintained an expression of gentle interest. He knew well that a story – a rather graphic editorial on the world – was bound to follow. She knew he would appreciate her rant, and he knew she would be in giggles very soon. Two hours later they were still talking, now less animated and lying in an embrace.

Maya and David had first encountered each other amidst a group of sixty-five on a train rolling through the Cascades. They had both been recent hires in the same studio of a large architecture firm, and had barely crossed one another in the first few months of being colleagues. The Dilbert-like cubicle landscape ensured that even the most collaborative of professionals behaved like frightened animals in burrows, emerging only to consume and relieve in response to bodily urges. *Talk about a cobbler's son with no shoes*, they'd laughed later. The studio had then taken a trip to Vancouver for an annual retreat, with the charge of getting to know one another better. *What a sham*, Maya had thought. Most people had made humdrum conversation – with Discovery Channel-style enquiries about curry and dowry, elephants and tigers, magicians and snake-charmers – anxious to sum-up this novel cultural specimen from the land of Gandhi (*Ghandi* to most Americans, to Maya's further aggravation), and oh, not to forget, also the land of the *Kamasutra*. Maya had mastered the art of concocting colorful stories for their unsuspecting consumption, and for her own private entertainment. Through the slew of heads, random small-talk, and the rhythmic chug-chug of the train, David had appeared out of the blue. There he was, in Maya's face, with the energy of a bullet. With barely any preamble, he had all but confronted her with a rapid-fire of questions about the partition of India, as if she might have personally interviewed Jinnah on the creation of Pakistan. Maya recalled having strong, mixed feelings; on the one hand she had been wooed and delighted, and on the other, she had wondered if this was humbug, an unabashed exploitation of a smattering of knowledge about her national heritage. They had proceeded to have a two-hour powwow, and Maya had left grudgingly impressed, still saying in her head: *Fucking Ivy-League Snob.*

Now lying in the crook of his arm Maya found it difficult to fit him quite so neatly into that initial characterization. *Of course he still is a snob*, she thought, stifling a giggle. "Why did you laugh?" David asked in his typical sleepy murmur. Maya was frequently amused at his never allowing a giggle, sigh or sniffle to slip by without enquiring about its specific purpose. "Oh, because you're such a snob," she answered. David smiled, opened one eye to raise his eyebrow in mock enquiry, and then closed it again. Maya closed her eyes too, and drifted into a deeper reminiscence. How she had enjoyed their mock quarrels; how they had reveled in relentless teasing to poke gentle fun at each other! How they had argued endlessly on controversial subjects, like two savvy lawyers practicing their favorite esoteric clauses, each outwitting the other at every turn, yet each taking secret delight in the other's battle victories, so that the bigger war of debate could carry on undeterred. Architecture. Science versus Art. Capitalism, Socialism, Communism. Religion and God. The English language and its idiosyncrasies. The State versus the Humble Man. Corporations. Democracy and War. The Odyssey, the Mahabharata. Marriage, Children, and Polygamy. Death. Reality and Illusion. Sex. Love.

Nearly one-and-a-half years had elapsed after that first exchange on the train, before Maya and David were assigned to the same project. Maya had been wary, certain that her creativity was about to be snuffed out by an arrogant, Roarkian idealist. Yet from the very beginning they played like two children in a sandbox together. Sand flew, eyes sparkled, ideas flowed, and energy crackled in the air. Everything was alive, and the sun seemed to shine brighter than usual. There was challenge, there were agreements and disagreements, there were irony and humor, and there was poignancy. The project was never built, but in the minds of David and Maya, the ideas had not perished. They were only in hibernation, to be tended back to life at the earliest opportunity. Someday. And so continued talks of boundless ideal projects. They were about architecture, but really they were manifestos on human life and society. David's mind was like a bottomless wellspring of ideas. Architecture was about humanity, civilization, and social reform. What was the ideal format for a truly valuable education of young children? What gave a people their ideal modern city? What kind of house symbolized the institution of marriage? *Someday the world would be a more refined place.* Maya loved the synaesthesia in creative expressions: where story meets architecture and architecture meets music. The poem as a painting of words. The building as a mystery, a keeper of secrets. Music and structure, sketch and prose, cooking and lovemaking. *Someday the world would be a more integrated place.*

Maya settled into a deeper snuggle, and heard David's eyelashes rustle as he opened his eyes. "Are you comfortable?" he asked gently, stroking silky, black strands off her face. Maya nodded into his chest. She recalled the other times when they weren't debating or exalting anything heroic, but talking solemnly about humble, little things. The memories of the first music lesson, of an asthmatic little sister, of the fright of quarreling parents. The memories of an unbefitting Christmas present, of a two-year-old's yellow hospital room, of a briefly missing brother. Sandcastles on a sub-tropical Indian seashore; midnight projects to make things in the woodshop. A singing competition; a wrestling match. Her childhood best-friend; his childhood best-friend. The first day of architecture school in Ahmedabad; the first day of architecture internship in Austin. A train journey to Bombay amidst riots; an automobile cruising through the natural wonders of the American Southwest. The petrichor from the first monsoons on Calcutta's parched earth, the vibrant, forceful cactus blooms of the Arizona desert. *History means thousands of years.* Maya promised David an architectural pilgrimage of India, someday. *Native ground means everything.* David promised Maya a road-trip to the remotest landscapes of America, someday. Often, when David had a thought and fumbled for the right words, Maya could telepathically complete his sentence; his unuttered thoughts mapped imagery onto her brain. Then there were the countless, delightful meals they had shared. How they loved the different cuisines, and how much excitement accompanied a newly discovered restaurant! And David had simply revered Maya's cooking. He had treated each meal with the reverence accorded to religious ritual, and had thanked her ceremoniously every time. Maya had always been surprised that the dish he loved the best was typically the simplest of preparations, the one she had thrown in as an afterthought, the one that might form the substance of a humble meal in remote Bengal. Often, after such feasting, they would speak of nothing at all. It was as if the deep contentment merited nothing short of complete, respectful silence. David would sit comfortably on Maya's silk rug, propped against the couch, reading from a book on her shelf. She would settle next to him with two cups of spiced chai, and he would begin reading select excerpts to her. Neither knew how or when the reading transitioned to Maya's singing. As Maya spontaneously sketched a favorite raga, David closed his eyes in meditation. *One could live two hundred years with a daily dose of raga,* he often said. Eventually there would be quiet again, but the communication never ceased; it continued through their synchronized breathing.

David's breathing was now regular; he was asleep. Maya often marveled at his sleep; it resembled a child's deeply peaceful slumber. She racked her brain to recall when and how they had started seeing each other all the time, no longer in larger groups of colleagues, but she couldn't quite lock the transition into place. And when had it become apparent that they were two halves of a *Rorschach*? When had she felt her world rock violently, as if she had encountered her mirror-soul? How could she know an alien as if from time immemorial, when she had grown into a mature adult in the opposite part of the world, shaped by a vastly different history, culture, experience and upbringing: all the things believed to be the formative forces of one's identity? What was her relationship to this person? Had they been twins, peas in a pod, or attached otherwise in a previous life? Or were they the fragmented halves of a star in the Heavens, scattered onto the earth's diametrically opposite sides as part of some cruelly devised experiment? What Maya had felt throbbing in her heartmind was far greater, far more expansive, far more overwhelming than what she had known in the past as love. This was an immense, indescribable force; it was also a startling reminder of her uncompromised creativity, of a deep desire for true purpose in this world. It summoned her to wake from the slumber of mediocrity, to act on her dreams, to not pale, to not lose courage. It was a staggering confrontation with her own spirit.

Then one day, like a ghost coming alive, Emily had reentered David's life. "I care for her, and she needs me right now," David had stated, as if that explained everything. The world that had felt beautifully integrated was now shattered, and Maya was left holding more than her share of the fragments. There had been months of darkness, a timeless eclipse. David had gone underground, a habit not entirely unknown to Maya; in other circumstances she had enjoyed calling him Heisenberg's quark, a particle whose location and momentum cannot be simultaneously determined. When Maya had occasionally caught him over the phone, he had chatted with her as if nothing extraordinary had transpired. He was buying a place in this dilapidated, Seattle neighborhood, rife with creative opportunities. *In my little Calcutta,* Maya hugged the thought. Finally, he was going to work for himself. *Someday little Calcutta will be transformed, lot by lot, with David's happy creations.* And he had always concluded their conversations with *Talk to you later.* Maya had no clear aspiration with which she had set out to see David again six days ago; which last story was left incomplete? Which idea remained to be debated, which dream was still to be envisioned? There she had stood, at the door to his new place. And David had asked nothing and explained nothing. He had simply accepted her by his side, like she had never once left it. And as they had huddled together like twins in a womb, they had never once mentioned Emily, not explicitly anyway. Her presence had just hung like dense, prickly air around them.

Now Maya rolled over to face away from David. He awoke and rolled with her, looping his other arm around her shoulders. "You're so quiet. What are you thinking?" he asked softly. "Oh, nothing," Maya replied, but in her heartmind a rapid-fire of vivid snapshots cycled through like a slide show. The Duwamish river flowing gently, with abandoned, dilapidated factory structures across its width, that make David's eyes gleam with delight. Someday that land will be his, and those structures will be given life once again. Old, crumbling parts of Calcutta in desperate want of revitalization, floating in Maya's mind as David exalts the promise of tomorrow, of someday. The deep-maroon bark of a Manzanita tree shining lusciously, one of only two in Seattle David says, and drives her out to see. A sweet scent wafting through her nostrils, from lavender that David plucks on a stroll, crushing it between his fingers and holding it up to her nose. And Maya could still inhale the intoxicating freshness of his body from that one time; she could still blink away the beads of sweat raining on her eyelids, still drown in the ecstasy, and still squirm vigorously from the fire that burned deep within her abdomen. Timeless hours of glory; streaming tears of heaven. Intertwining of tendrils; clutching of heartstrings. A union of twinsouls; a meeting of heartminds. A swirling mix of hues … Maya could no longer stand the knot forming in her belly. "I'm going on a trip," she announced abruptly, her voice cutting through the stillness. "Where to?" "Yellowstone." Maya could feel David break into a warm smile on the back of her neck. "Let me show you something, then!" He gently extricated himself and returned moments later with what looked like three large rolls of canvas. He let them unfurl on the carpet like displays of ochre silk in an Indian sari store. They were the finest geological maps of three American states: Wyoming, Arizona, and California. With his forefinger, he gleefully traced the boundaries of Yellowstone Park, his eyes now fully alert with pride and delight in the abundant, natural riches of his country.

Then David's finger found the Arizona desert. "I refuse to see that on a map," Maya pouted, half serious, half mocking. "Alright, point noted," David's shoulders fell in slight regret, his eyes softened, and he touched her forehead gingerly where she might wear a bindi. "Just like the architecture pilgrimage of India," Maya continued, not hoping for anything. "Yes, just like that," David responded. "So you *will* explore India with me, then?" Maya exclaimed, throwing her arms around his neck and pulling him towards the floor in an unexpected display of the old, familiar exuberance, her shoulder skimming the edges of the beautiful maps lying unrolled on the carpet. "Yes," David said softly, with a smile. "Someday?" she asked, also smiling. "Mm-hmm," he murmured, the smile deepening in his eyes to mirror hers, as it always did. He was aware of her teasing. "And if I were to die before that? Become a star in the sky, you know, the brightest ever?" "Then I will journey with your ashes to India and scatter them over the Ganges," David said somewhat solemnly. Maya started to laugh out loud. "And will you shave your head for me as well?" "Yes! Someday, not tomorrow, but someday," David was grinning again. "Alright, then! We'll begin with the seven cities of Delhi, proceed to the stepped wells of Gujarat, move through the golden sands and grand palaces of Rajasthan, further to the rock caves of Madhya Pradesh and Maharashtra, and then head south to see all the stone temples." "Including the rock-cut ones on the sea-shore, your childhood playground?" David prodded. "Mahabalipuram," Maya nodded, her eyes now closed, her head on the floor. David's fingers absently traced small circles on her right temple. "Then we'll see the stone chariot in Orissa, the tigers of Bengal, and the remote hills of Sikkim," Maya continued. "Inhabited by Indian-Chinese?" David prompted again, knowing she would giggle at this reference. "Mm-hmm," answered Maya, smiling with her eyes still closed. "I'll hold you to your word then, David!" she said, remnants of laughter still lacing her voice, but gradually turning wistful. "Someday," she answered herself on his behalf in a low whisper, almost with wonderment. The deeper secret, the more profound truth that had lingered in the air all evening, now stood naked. *Parallel lines only meet at infinity.*

David buried his face next to hers, and they stayed in a loose embrace for long, silent moments. "Give me a kiss then, and I shall be off," Maya said finally, her tone almost casual. David kissed her gently, barely skimming her lips with his. A part of Maya arched for more, like a dying man grasping at final gasps of air, but the core of her remained present with the profundity of truth. They had together made an unspoken pact to resuscitate their connection through the beautiful mirage of possibility, in outrageous denial of bare, obvious, staring-in-the-face fact. Maya lay motionless with her eyes closed, calming her breath. Then she disentangled herself from him and pranced down the stairs with an inexplicable levity, straight into the chilly night. David followed, his footsteps tentative in surprise at the suddenness of her exit. Maya's eyes were dazzling onyxes as she looked at him from the driver's seat of her car, and he poked his head through the passenger-side window, returning her gaze with beaming sapphires. "Talk to you later," David said with his unfailing, boyish eagerness. Maya smiled knowingly, turning David's *Talk to you later* round and round in her head like concrete slush in a mixer. How much he liked to say that. *Later. Tomorrow. Someday.* As she pressed down on the accelerator and pulled away, Maya made a desperate bid to brand the image of David's eyes into the deepest folds of her memory. That beautiful, bottomless blue, which had so lovingly and completely cradled the purest reflection of her soul. Pulling away, Maya was powerfully aware of the undeniable truth, the certainty of her own determination, of the venerable finality of this instance. A staggering sense of loss overwhelmed her, as if half her soul were departing her body. In that moment she knew she would never be seeing David again. Or as he would have preferred to say it: not until *someday.*

8

Autumn

The summer of 1998 came and went as Shibani watched from the sole window in the tiny studio. It was six months, almost, since she had arrived in this small, remote foreign town, only three weeks after the wedding. The wedding ... the sights and sounds of hundreds of people, her father running around frantically to make all the arrangements, her mother looking harried and relieved at once ... it all seemed so recent, yet so distant. Shibani recalled the wobbliness in her legs and the thumping of her heart through the five days of rituals, feasts and celebrations. The match had been finalized at express speed; the boy was a PhD student in the United States, and had only so much time off at his disposal. His parents had wanted the "alliance" to be settled and the wedding ceremony to take place, all in a matter of days. They had come to see Shibani on January twenty-first, and the wedding date had been set for February fifteenth.

The next few days had been the craziest frenzy in which Shibani had ever seen her parents. A venue and priest had to be found, wedding cards had to be printed, five hundred people, no less, had to be invited, jewelry had to be bought, saris had to be selected, the catering had to be organized, gifts for everyone in the boy's family had to be chosen. And through all this, Shibani could only sit immobile, with a lump in her throat. At times she had felt like an external observer of this stampede of events: distant, remote, almost uncaring. At other times, feelings of sadness, fear, and a terrible sense of finality had gripped her heart. She was to be married to a stranger, and travel miles and miles away from her family to the land of plenty, the United States of America.

Shibani woke from her reverie as raindrops splattered the glass like marbles scattering on a polished floor. She was tired of waiting for the mailman each afternoon. Perhaps there would be a letter for her? Surely her mother had dropped her a line? Or maybe her sister had mailed a recent picture of her newborn daughter, or a copy of her son's preschool scribbles? She had been so excited to receive Shobhana's last letter over a month ago, which had concluded with "Dear Mashi, I miss you," in the obviously adult-guided scribble of a young child. Shibani vividly remembered the day Shobhana was married; at that time she had just felt like an excited child, thrilled at all the festivities, unsuspecting of the feelings in her older sister's heart. Had she felt quite as gripped with fear and uncertainty as Shibani had felt at her own wedding five years later? It hadn't seemed so; Shobhana was always so composed, and in control of herself. As their parents always said, "Shobhana is picture-perfect."

Anil was not a bad man, really. In those hurried days of the wedding and in the paraphernalia of marriage rituals and gear, all Shibani had caught were fleeting glimpses of a rather mouse-like man with a thin moustache, and an angular jaw beneath the long topor that crowned his head. Now, six months later, Shibani thought that she knew her husband somewhat well. He was nice at most times and cared adequately for her basic needs, frequently taking on a manner of parental concern. Had she stowed her glasses away safely in the drawer? Had she wrapped her head in a scarf on this slightly chilly September night, when they set out to buy their weekly groceries? Oh, and he needed to buy her a winter-coat soon; the Illinois winter was hardly going to be warded off by the jacket her parents had bought her from Sarojini Nagar in Delhi! Anil clicked his tongue rhythmically whenever mildly annoyed, such as while writing checks for monthly bills. He also raised his eye-brows in a quizzical expression when talking on the phone, as if asking an endless question of the person on the other side of the line, to which there could be no satisfactory answer. He slurped his dal-bhat loudly at dinner, and his mouth hung slightly open while watching the news on television. Anil was a creature of habit, and always did the same thing at the same time. He left the apartment exactly at 8:00am for the Everitt Engineering Lab, and arrived home exactly at 12:30pm for lunch. He left just as promptly at 1:15pm after a quick glimpse of CNN's midday news, and returned at 8:30pm. They ate dinner at 9:00pm sitting in front of the television, watching a couple of shows and more news. At bed-time his robotic manner became acute. Every night Anil changed into his pajamas, washed up with great rigor and discipline in the bathroom, put on his night socks, and turned to face Shibani. At this cue they copulated in complete silence, and Anil was snoring gently by 11pm. Shibani lay awake afterwards, staring at the patterns on the ceiling, cast by the occasional car's lights filtering through the twisted blinds in their single window.

Shibani had her routine too. She awoke with Anil at 6:30am, and got busy in their tiny, single-counter kitchen making cha. He liked dipping biscuits in his tea, and Shibani had discovered graham crackers to be the best substitute for the Glucose or Marie biscuits of their childhood. As he dutifully performed his morning ablutions she fixed breakfast, either of eggs and toast, or a hot cereal. Anil had his breakfast and a second round of tea over snapshots of the morning news, and left for work. Shibani, at this time, was usually still sipping her first cup of tea. She watched Anil walk down their street, cross it, then disappear behind tall evergreens, his billowing sport-jacket following his thin legs into oblivion. After her breakfast Shibani showered, and watched a morning run of old mystery shows on A&E. *Quincy* was followed by *Murder She Wrote*. This signaled that it was time to quickly fix lunch, which was usually made up of leftovers from the previous night. After Anil left, Shibani joined *Law & Order* fifteen minutes late. Time drifted into *Columbo*, which ran for two hours, and portrayed a bumbling detective of Italian descent sporting an old, beige raincoat and solving the most scientifically constructed murder-mysteries. Shibani was still learning to pick up the American accent and didn't follow many of the lines, especially if they had colloquialisms or cultural references. It was almost three in the afternoon when Columbo successfully nabbed yet another cleverly scheming murderer, and so, it was time to watch for the mailman over an afternoon cup of tea. After ascertaining that the mail had no letters for her, Shibani usually set out on a reconnaissance of the refrigerator for contents that would make up dinner. She cooked for about an hour-and-a-half, turning on some Rabindrasangeet, or oldies from Hindi films such as *Best of Lata* or *Best of Kishore* from Anil's tape collection, as a backdrop for her culinary ventures. Around five Shibani took an ambulatory walk around the neighborhood for about half-an-hour. Thus passed day after day, week after week, and month after month.

* * * * *

On one of those brightly-colored autumn Saturdays Anil suggested uncharacteristically, that they take a road trip to Chicago. He didn't like driving on the highways very much; finding the correct exits always made him agitated. Chicago is where Shibani had entered America for the first time, trailing Anil timidly in her sari, among the sea of foreign people in the expansive O'Hare International Airport. The people had looked bigger, the immigration officials stronger, the light brighter, and the air cleaner than each of their Indian counterparts. There seemed to be more of everything, a plentifulness: a quality instantly recognizable in this alien land. But, of course, after thirty-two hours of travel and nine hours of jetlag, they had driven directly to Urbana-Champaign and had not ventured into Chicago. Anil's roommates, Shounak and Ravi, had been there to pick them up in Ravi's eleven-year-old, dusty, 1986 Honda Civic. The three-hour drive had felt like yet another dream; Shounak and Ravi had sported curiously suggestive smiles, Anil had assumed a defensive manner, and Shibani had sat in a stupor in the backseat, watching plain after plain in dull yellows pass by.

Now they were going to drive that route again, towards one of the most famous cities in the world. Shibani knew very little about Chicago; all she could recall was that a great fire had caused much of it to be rebuilt; "Just like London two-hundred years prior," her history teacher had explained. Anil was rather officious at the rental car office, and when a pet cat suddenly landed on the counter he burst into a volley of clicking sounds, agitated by this unexpected divergence from his expectations. They were awarded a shiny white car; it was a Chevrolet, Anil informed Shibani, which was to her at once nondescript and special. The smell of new plastic engulfed them as they buckled up for the drive. Anil carefully unfolded the map given to them by the rental agency, and studied it like a schoolboy. He nodded to himself, and asked Shibani to spread the map across her lap. Then they set off across the plains, occasionally punctuated by a grain silo that had a bright yellow smiley-face painted on it. The landscape advanced and receded, then advanced and receded, and gave Shibani the feeling of a meditative timelessness. In spite of the high speeds, time seemed to slow to a standstill, and the mind, once again, became the objective observer to a set of events outside its control.

After exactly three hours and twelve minutes Anil pulled into a parking garage a few blocks from the Sears Tower. "It's the tallest building in the world!" Anil announced with pride, like he had had something to do with its conception. Shibani stared up the glass of the exterior; the tall, slender tower looked down at her menacingly, and like the immense, receding landscapes they had driven by, its peak disappeared elusively into the sky. They stood in disciplined lines at the ticket counter, and were finally ushered into a spacious elevator with a friendly assistant. He gave them the history of the tower in the six minutes it took to reach the viewing deck at the top, but Shibani could hear nothing through the popping in her ears. At the deck, the city of Chicago exploded all around them in shades of blue-gray. People thronged at the periphery, posing to take pictures, aiming telescopes at Lake Michigan; couples kissed, kids jumped, and older people made aimless rounds. Shibani was startled to see two large groups of Indians: one, a family of parents, kids and grandparents, and another, quite obviously a group of young graduate students from one of the many nearby universities. Then she spotted a third party: a couple shyly holding hands, the woman's forearms jingling with colorful glass bangles, and the parting in her hair beaming with bright-red sindoor. They must be newly married, she thought. Shibani felt a heart-tugging kinship to all of these strangers from her homeland, yet she averted her eyes when passing them by.

Later Anil took Shibani to Devon Street, the "Little India" of Chicago. Shibani felt nearly faint with shock. Wide American streets ended abruptly and narrow Indian gallis took over. The usual intersection was replaced by a chowraha, replete with the betel-leaf-chewing newspaper vendor, and the scrotum-scratching, idle by-stander. *Gandhi Electronics – 220 Volts* screamed one neon sign in electric blue. Sequincovered chiffon saris clung seductively to white and black mannequins in grimy show-windows. The smells of frying bhaturas and browning dosas intermingled into a single, oily olfactory experience, making Shibani at once nauseated and ravenous. They walked into Udipi Café for a late lunch. The green, marbled, plastic table-tops surrounded by plastic chairs, in which countless people sat slurping sambars and rasams with their dosas, the pink walls with Mughal cusped-arches carved in relief to create niches, and the numerous waiters bumping into each other in their zealous effort to serve the same table, all transported Shibani directly to a street-café in one of Delhi's lively lanes, minus the thirty-two-hour journey. She had fallen into a magic hole in the earth, like Alice in Wonderland, and made a transition that required the passing of neither time nor distance, enabling an instantaneous passage through a threshold into another, intensely familiar world. The soapy, air-freshening, disinfecting smells of America had instantly evaporated, and had been replaced by the pungency of Indian smells, scents and odors. The largeness, expansiveness and sparseness of everything American had been replaced by the smallness and density of everything Indian. Shibani sat nibbling her crisp paper-dosa, and could not take her eyes off all the people around her. Back on the road to Urbana-Champaign she found it impossible to align the sensory experiences in the two worlds – the intense dosa place and the quiet, endless landscape – into a single reference-frame of time and space.

* * * * *

The next day life in Anil and Shibani's studio resumed as abruptly as the chasm between Devon Street and the rest of America. Two rounds of tea, breakfast, watching Anil disappear and reappear, news channels and mysteries, cooking and waiting for the mail … all continued like clockwork. This went on day after day, until one afternoon when entering the apartment building from her 5:00pm walk, Shibani was nearly run over in the lobby by a young chap with a bicycle, wearing a damp jacket and stumbling through the doors of the building. Beyond the fringe of his hood, Shibani could see tousled, curly, reddish hair. "Sorry," he said in a thick accent, and grinned sheepishly. "You are Indian?" he asked. Shibani nodded without a word; she was not sure quite what to say. "I am Jean-Claude, and I live here too. I study art and art history at the university," the friendly, hooded man said, extending his hand. Shibani took it shyly, and said, "I am Shibani. I am living in 302 with my husband for the past six months." Jean-Claude grinned again, and then motioned towards the elevator. He pressed #3 for Shibani, and #5 for himself. Shibani said bye and left the elevator cab with a hurried step. She had never before talked to a stranger in America, other than at the check-out line of the 24-hour grocery store!

That afternoon Shibani couldn't focus on Columbo's attempt to trap a deceptive TV chef, who had cleverly poisoned his on-show guest while the cameras were rolling, and had still managed to manufacture an alibi. She was rather pleased with herself for having boldly shaken hands with a stranger, but was embarrassed that she had told him her apartment number. She wondered what it would be like to study art or art history in an American university. She had studied political science at Delhi University for her Bachelor's degree, and there had been references to the crossovers in art and political movements in history, but it had not occurred to her to tell Jean-Claude all this while introducing herself. Being a Bengali, Shibani of course knew Tagore's music, writings and paintings, but not very much more about art in general. Now it made her think back to all her college studies and wonder why she had spent three long years reading and writing, and taking difficult tests. Why had she learned all that she had? What relevance did those times have now? Shibani was restless with these thoughts and couldn't focus on her cooking. She forgot the salt in the dal, and realized this only when Anil made clicking sounds at the dinner table that night. Later, through the silent copulation, Shibani's mind swirled with images of important political figures making lavish paintings with rich, thick and vibrant earth colors. Tagore's music was splattered all over rolls of canvas in hues of blue, yellow and red. His short stories were little sequences of entry, arrival and exit from grand buildings. Deeply absorbed in such imagery, she didn't remotely feel Anil go limp next to her and begin his gentle snoring.

The following day Shibani found herself looking out for Jean-Claude when leaving for her routine walk. And sure enough he appeared magically like an answer from the universe, with his hooded coat, bicycle and all. "Taking a walk?" he asked cheerfully. As Shibani nodded, he added, "May I walk with you?" Shibani could hardly contain her excitement at the prospect of asking Jean-Claude all about his art-history coursework. "Where are you from?" she asked timidly, as they broke into a walk together, Jean-Claude wheeling his bicycle over the rustling, multicolored autumn leaves on the moist ground. "I am French!" he replied with enthusiasm. They walked with Jean-Claude's bicycle between them like a little geographic boundary on wheels, separating India and France on American soil. Shibani asked him what he was currently studying in his courses. *History-Theory-and-Criticism, Ceramics, Life Drawing, Renaissance Art, Introduction to Art in Architecture* ... everything sounded fascinating to Shibani. Her mind drifted to the references of the Renaissance in her political science classes back in college, trying to dig up the faded memories. As they strolled along Green Street, past Anil's Everitt Lab and towards the dividing line between the twin towns Urbana and Champaign, Jean-Claude asked Shibani if she would like a cup of coffee. Again Shibani found herself tongue-tied. The last time she had had coffee with anybody other than Anil or her family was back in her college days, when on rainy afternoons a gang of classmates would hang out together around the campus dhaba, sipping Nescafe from small, chipped ceramic cups. Shyly, she moved her head in the characteristically Indian affirmative nod, the complex combination of head-, neck- and eye-movements that act in concert to acknowledge or acquiesce. Jean-Claude seemed to have no trouble following, and he led them into a light and airy coffee shop with tall ceilings and exposed structure. Shibani felt the expansiveness of the space fill her body, instantly lifting her out of the constriction of the small apartment in which she spent most of her time. The spot behind the ordering counter was shiny and happy, with coffee machines and grinders, cups hanging off racks, and tall, colored bottles of flavored syrup. Shibani ordered an Americano since it was the only coffee drink Anil had ordered for her before. "Room for cream?" the barista asked. Shibani looked blankly at Jean-Claude, and he explained that she was asking whether to leave space in the cup for adding cream or milk to the coffee. Shibani nodded again silently, grateful for his help, and Jean-Claude relayed her response to the tattooed woman across the counter. For himself he ordered one of those syrupy Italian sodas, and Shibani thought to herself that she would try one next time. Then she was embarrassed to realize that she had walked out of the apartment without her wallet; she had never previously needed money on her walks; when she was out with Anil he always handled all transactions anyway. But Jean-Claude was already settling the bill. "Thank you," Shibani said from behind lowered eyes. "No problem, Shibani!" he said, and she blushed at his taking her name. She noticed for the first time that despite his unkempt look Jean-Claude had a becoming, warm face. His hazel-green eyes sparkled with energy and perhaps, mischief. They sat at a bar table and Shibani's salwar-clad legs dangled awkwardly from her high perch. As they sipped their drinks conversation gradually returned. "How much longer for your studies to be completed?" Shibani asked, and they continued to chat. An hour-and-half later Jean-Claude announced that he was going to the library, and Shibani, startled that so much time had flown by, walked home hurriedly to finish the rest of her preparation and cooking for dinner.

* * * * *

The days and weeks of autumn followed, and every day Shibani eagerly anticipated her afternoon walk. She forgot all about the mailman, and the fretful watching and waiting for letters. She didn't bother with the afternoon shows on television, or worry much about what to cook for dinner. Promptly at five o'clock she set out for her walk. Sometimes Jean-Claude showed up and at other times he didn't. When he did they drank coffee or visited the library, or walked along the strip of shops looking in the windows, or simply traipsed through campus exploring the buildings. Jean-Claude introduced her to all the campus sections: the John Bardeen engineering quad and the neighboring Beckman Institute with its shiny green glass and precise brickwork, the large central quad, the main library, the Art+Design and Architecture buildings, the Medical and Life Sciences buildings, the elegant Krannert Center where they showed studio plays. Once he even took her to the Krannert Art Museum. Shibani loved thinking of all these sections of campus as different houses of knowledge, where people from all over the world came together to learn about various subjects and about each other. She yearned to share in that experience. Each time they sat down to chat in the coffee shop Jean-Claude asked her more about her family back in India, about her life growing up, about her hobbies, her school and college ... and as she filled in the puzzle for him piece-by-piece in various sections, she could see in her mind's eye her own life forming into a complete picture. And every time she tried to integrate Anil into this picture, he felt like a discontinuous piece, a piece that didn't correctly fit the puzzle anywhere, jarring in its forced efforts to join in, like a tumor on clean, smooth edges.

On the afternoons that Jean-Claude didn't show up in the apartment lobby Shibani felt disappointed, but she still went on her walks. She pretended Jean-Claude was along anyway, asking her as usual, "Where do you want to go today, Shibani?" And she answered him in her mind, then set off to wherever she pleased. Sometimes she was even bold enough to stray from the paths they had traversed together. She wondered if she would run into Anil somewhere on campus, but the slave to routine that he was, she doubted that he ever broke his pattern to go anywhere but to his classes and back to his office. On some days she spent an hour or more at the library, touching the books, opening the journals and simply enjoying the wonderful space. As the leaves continued to fall off the trees around her, Shibani too began to shed her shyness and her dependence on the structured life with Anil at its center. She was now almost bare, like a nude tree ready to grow new leaves, like a blank canvas ready to be painted on. Her step was light, and the rustle of beautiful yellow, brown and red leaves underneath added music to her gait.

The season progressed and the air transformed to acquire a pleasing moistness reminiscent of the Delhi air when it was time for Shibani's favorite time of the year: Durga Puja followed by Diwali. Taking deep breaths to savor the scent in the air, she told Jean-Claude all about the festivals. She remembered to him the various impressions of Goddess Durga and her entourage created all over the city's neighborhoods, each competing with the next in its creativity, artistry and craftsmanship. The best spots were usually in the Bengali stronghold of Chittaranjan Park. The proud residents milled about in new clothes eating sweets, and exchanging gifts and greetings. The streets were chock full of goodies; Shibani's favorites were the kathi rolls and biryani. A few weeks after Goddess Durga left earth again by immersing herself in the holy waters of the Yamuna or Ganga, the skies were ablaze with fireworks to celebrate Diwali, the day of Lord Rama's return to Ayodhya after his long exile.

Delhi residents flocked to the various open-air grounds and theaters to watch the *Rama Lila*, and set alight monumental effigies of the demon Ravana. "Aren't you going to celebrate?" Jean-Claude asked her upon hearing these vivid descriptions. "I don't even know when the festivals are this year!" Shibani answered, feeling sad. Anil had not mentioned anything about the festival dates; since they changed each year according to the lunar calendar, it was impossible to know without making a special effort. Jean-Claude promptly took her to one of the computer terminals in the library to search for the information. Shibani was fascinated by what the Internet could do; simply entering keywords on a website called Google turned up all the details she needed! They found out that Durga Puja was already in ashthami, the eighth day of its ten-day cycle. "I must write to my parents soon to convey my Bijoya regards!" she exclaimed. Diwali, they noted, was in about two weeks, at the end of October. When the day came around, Shibani lit little candles all over the apartment, and made sweets of condensed milk. In place of their afternoon walk she asked Jean-Claude to come by her apartment to try some of her sweets, trembling with delight over their own private celebration. Diwali even coincided with the American festival Halloween. On their walk the next day Jean-Claude showed her how people carved big, bright-orange pumpkins into faces and lit candles inside them, and Shibani marveled at how these pumpkin-lanterns created an atmosphere that beautifully echoed the moods of her own festival running concurrently.

* * * * *

A month passed by and it was beginning to get too cold to walk outside for too long at a time, so Shibani and Jean-Claude spent more time chatting indoors in the coffee shop or library. Shibani could no longer recall her life in America without Jean-Claude, and their sharing of stories and laughter. Occasionally it occurred to her that she knew him — replete with his thoughts, feelings, ideas and dreams — better than she knew her husband, even though they shared no cultural background or personal history. Soon it was time for Thanksgiving, the major American holiday. Anil suggested they visit his uncle – his father's cousin – a doctor who lived in the suburbs of Chicago in a large, comfortable house. Anil assumed this would be happy news to Shibani, but she found herself feeling entirely uninterested; she wanted to stay in Urbana-Champaign and have Jean-Claude teach her all about this holiday too. But she went along silently, to the rental car place with the pet cat, through the advancing and receding plains, and into the big city and big house of this doctor-uncle. With aunty affectionately cooking traditional Bengali meals, uncle offering exploratory rides through the city, and their cute little daughters grabbing at Shibani's arms for attention, this would've been Shibani's dream come true in those terribly isolating, early months in America. But now she was distracted, even somewhat annoyed. Images of walks, libraries, books, art, coffee … and colorful, rustling leaves floated in her mind.

When they returned to their studio in Urbana, Shibani could hardly wait for the next time she would take a walk with Jean-Claude. There was no sign of him the following day, so Shibani walked by herself, even venturing into the café and drinking a cup of coffee alone for the first time in her life. Perhaps he too had left town for the long weekend; she was sure she would find Jean-Claude the next day. But day after day went by and there was no sign of him. Shibani searched every square-inch of campus, looking around every building and every street corner. She scoured the library repeatedly. She even walked all the way to the Arts building; there was no Jean-Claude. After five long days of waiting and searching, Shibani could no longer find it in herself to take the afternoon walks. She sat in the apartment gazing out the window and watching for the mailman, warm tears rolling down silently on her cheeks. Outside, the air was quickly turning wintry and the days were getting shorter, nightfall unexpectedly blackening out Shibani's sole window-view. Inside, Kishore

Kumar was singing in his heartrending, melodious voice through Anil's cassette-tape player, "*Aane vaala pal, jaane vaala hai; ho sake to isme, zindagi bitalo, pal jo yeh jaane vaala hai...*"

The moment to come shall also pass;

Live, if you will, a whole life in this instant:

In this moment that is soon to pass.

One moment, I encounter an innocent bud;

Blooming, it says: I'm off to another form.

Look – and it's right here, search – and it's nowhere:

Live, if you will, a whole life in this instant:

In this moment that is soon to pass.

Now, a moment falls from time,

It holds a rich story... but see, the moment has passed;

With a few laughs and a few tears,

Live, if you will, a whole life in this instant:

In this moment that is soon to pass.

That night, when Anil turned to her wordlessly in bed, Shibani turned away and curled into a tight ball. She said in a low but firm voice,

"No. I want to sleep." And then a few moments later, "I want to apply to graduate school. I want to study art and art history." Anil made throaty, clicking sounds, but they bounced off her back. Shibani knew where the application forms were in the library. Tomorrow she was going to apply to the graduate program in the School of Art+Design.

9

The Dollhouse

I am nine-and-a-half years old. I will be a full ten years old in May. I think I'm close to being grown up now. We are living for one year in Germany, because Daddy has been invited by the Humboldt Foundation to stay here, and write an important Physics book. He says that my name and little Arjun's name and Mamma's name will all be in it, on the front page! We are going to German school. The kids there are so big. They bully me, and steal my orange juice at break time. I think to myself that I look dark and small and forgotten among them.

Uncle and Aunty have become good friends of my parents. I like Uncle a lot because he is fun, and he has built a wonderful wooden dollhouse for his daughter, who is my age and my friend. The dollhouse has beds and tables and chairs, and little dressed-up dolls. It even has lights for night time! Uncle and Aunty and their daughter and son live not too far away from our apartment in this little town. So, we go there often in our Audi 800. I tell my friend that her father is my favorite Uncle among all the Indian uncles here.

Daddy is invited to travel for three weeks on a fully-paid tour of Germany. Mamma is invited to go along with him. Daddy is very excited about this, but he and Mamma are arguing about whether she should go along or not. Children are not allowed, so Arjun and I will have to stay behind. I am really frightened. They decide to go, and leave us in the care of Uncle and Aunty.

We are staying at home with a babysitter, Nicole, who is seventeen years old, and either Uncle or Aunty is supposed to visit us every evening. Nicole is funny. She cannot eat any spice in her food; she adds hardly any salt in the boiled potatoes. And she gets fully naked before getting in bed in my parents bedroom! In the day time we have school. On the weekends, we are supposed to stay at Uncle and Aunty's house, so that Nicole can have a break. I am happily waiting for the weekend, because I can play with my friend and with her lovely dollhouse. But I am so afraid all week when Mamma and Daddy are not here in the apartment. I cry, and cannot sleep or do my homework.

Arjun gets a bad attack of asthma. He has got these attacks since he was a little baby. Mamma says he gets them whenever Daddy is away, which is a lot of the time. I am so afraid. Uncle comes to see us, and to make sure Arjun is okay. Arjun is in the bedroom. Since I am growing up, and Mamma has taught me to make tea for grown-ups, I am making some tea for Uncle in the kitchen. He is now standing in front of me. He asks me, "You like Uncle, don't you?" I feel shy, and a bit scared. He pulls me to him and begins to push his face into mine. I don't know why he is doing this. Then he puts his big lips on my mouth, and spits all over my mouth. He starts to open my mouth with his mouth, and puts his tongue inside. My lips are burning and I am feeling suffocated. He is pushing harder and harder. The water for tea is boiling.

Uncle now comes to the apartment every evening. When the bell rings, I peer through the peep-hole, and I feel scared. After seeing Arjun and leaving him to play with his toys in the bedroom, he finds me and takes me to the living room. He puts me on his knee and begins to do those strange things again. Nowadays he rubs my thigh, and puts his hand into my skirt. And he puts his hands on my chest and rubs hard and pinches hard. I don't know why he does this, but it hurts a lot. Sometimes, I cannot run or play the next day in school because of the pain. On the weekends we are in their house, and when we have finished dinner and are getting ready for bedtime, Arjun and my friend and her brother are all in the kids' room. Aunty is in the kitchen, washing dishes in a sink of foam, wearing yellow gloves on her hands. Uncle finds me in the kids' room or bathroom or hallway, and brings me to the living room. He puts me on his lap, and does the same things again. I am afraid that Aunty will see and scold me badly, and tell my parents. I am also sad that I cannot play with the dollhouse.

Daddy and Mamma return from their trip. They are very worried about Arjun. He gets better soon after they are back. I am afraid they will find out my bad secret. I am afraid because I know I have done something wrong. I cannot sleep at night. But they don't find out. One day in school I find that I am bleeding in my panties. I am afraid to tell Mamma about this because I think I have cancer from all the wrong things I have been doing, and Mamma will cry if she hears that I am going to die. But after many times of bleeding and dirty panties, I just have to tell her. She cries for a long time, so now I *know* I have cancer and I'm going to die. But later she tells me that I am grown up now and have eggs in my tummy, which have to leave my body once a month and come out of my pee-hole. I have to wear something like a diaper in those days of the month. When Uncle and Aunty visit, Uncle pulls me to a corner and whispers to me, "So you have grown up now!" I feel dirty, and very angry with Mamma for telling them about my eggs and blood.

We live in Germany for five more months before returning to India. Uncle and Aunty visit many times, and Uncle finds me in the bedroom every time. I am always afraid that Mamma and Daddy will find out and scold me badly, but they never find out. *I am grown up now.* These days I notice other people, especially on TV, putting their mouths together. They seem to like it, but I know how horrible it is to have burning lips and spit in your mouth. Daddy doesn't like me to watch all this, so I *know* that I have done something terribly wrong.

Back in India ... I do not have a dollhouse. I think of the dollhouse for a long time. I wish Daddy would build me a dollhouse, so I can play once again.

10

Sexodrome

Waiting at Charles de Gaulle for her flight home to Seattle, Anamika had a warm tranquility enveloping her even amidst the confusion and hubbub of a major international airport. She felt whole, as if the lacunae of self-doubt and loathing that had permeated her being for so long had been filled, leaving only their faint edges, soon to be entirely erased. The core between her legs still throbbed happily, her guts felt satiated with gastronomic delights, and her mind continuously replayed images of beautiful buildings, the artists of Montmartre, and the boulevards full of cafés and languishing Parisians. But those things were only the backdrop to the center-stage; it was her spirit that reigned supreme in the foreground, centered, conscious, creative. Less than seventy-two hours earlier when she had arrived in Paris, she hadn't had the faintest idea that such aliveness and equanimity could be possible.

* * * * *

Anamika felt winded. She was running to the gate after the harrowing security line at SeaTac airport, with the heavy laptop case cutting painfully into her left shoulder, and one of those ubiquitous rolling bags dragging behind on the right. With progressively heightening levels of threat, her name was ricocheting through the airport via the public announcement system: "All passengers proceed to Gate 13 for departure of Air France 309 … Ms. Anamika Saha, please proceed to Gate 13 immediately … Ms. Anamika Saha, your flight is ready for departure … Ms. Anamika Saha your gate will close in three minutes …" It was a public humiliation; red-faced and panting, Anamika imagined that every passenger she scurried by in the airport could identify her as the culprit, rolling their eyes and passing judgment at her irresponsibility. Yet, when actually faced with the heaving, breathless Anamika, the attendants at the gate managed to sport perky smiles and reassuring nods, as if they had had nothing whatsoever to do with the series of warnings. The second she dropped into her seat the plane began to roll back. She groped for her seatbelt, leaned back into the headrest, and closed her eyes.

It wasn't that Anamika was a novice at this. Making it through tedious and cumbersome post-9/11 security procedures in time to catch flights, that is. She'd been traveling incessantly for business in the last eight years, first domestically and then internationally; she'd made five whirlwind trips to Hong Kong alone in the last nine months, and at least two to London. But it was a different Anamika taking off this time; the certainty, predictability and practiced self-assuredness of her professional aspect were abruptly replaced by the uncertainty, vulnerability and alarming rawness of a debutante. On a total whim, she was headed to Paris for a weekend, to "clear her head," she had told her baffled friends. It had required her to expend a new kind of effort to get to the airport and on the plane; she was painfully aware of the resistance, the nagging voices, the fear. She could breeze through high-level presentations to corporate executives of multinational real-estate companies, developers and civic authorities, but she was entirely unsettled and discombobulated on this little jaunt to Paris.

And, it wasn't that Anamika was afraid of being alone, either. In fact it was her forte, something her large circle of loyal friends openly admired. At forty-two, she had been alone a long time, faraway from her parents and extended family in India, accustomed to being comfortably cocooned in her spacious downtown apartment with concrete floors and spectacular views of Puget Sound and Mt. Rainier, expertly taking care of life's everyday, earthly matters of existence and subsistence. It was over matters of the heart that she had no grasp whatsoever, and this particular failing boomeranged repeatedly into her life to mess with her, probe her, test her, and expose her, leaving her in distress and confusion. They were always different – white men, brown men, a black man once – but it always ended the same way: with angry accusations, protestations and the inevitable parting of ways. "What a huge and unnecessary price to pay for sex!" Anamika lamented afterwards to her friends, who nodded loyally, but never quite understood.

She opened her eyes, and rolled them promptly at what she encountered in her immediate field of vision. The plane had taxied to the runway and was now taking off, and in the seats in front of her, an older couple was holding hands across the aisle, their speckled, wrinkled, leathery arms dangling in a V-shape and knotted in the center with tightly clasped hands, roping off the aisle like portions of the security line that Anamika had just madly thrashed through for an hour. *Aaaaaaaaawww*, she thought cynically, even bitterly. *See, this is what I just don't get.* How on earth did people get to years and years of togetherness, past the arguments and the kids and the Costco lists and the habitual nitpicking and grinding boredom of daily togetherness … and then want to hold hands across an airplane aisle for take-off … at age sixty-something? How *did* they do it?

She must have unwittingly voiced some part of this diatribe, for her co-passenger in the window seat started, and smiled at her nervously. Anamika offered up a smile in return, deciding to relax into a less disagreeable demeanor, and chit-chatted a bit with the lean blonde next to her. Lise was returning to her family in Germany after a three-month forestry internship in the Cascade Mountains, and was first stopping in Paris to see a friend. How beautiful the Pacific Northwest is! How wonderful the forest rangers are! What a lovely city Seattle is! Young Lise leaned forward with untarnished, earnest enthusiasm, her gangly arms twisting and turning in pleasure as she talked. Anamika nodded politely for a bit, and then nodded off to sleep.

* * * * *

The little dark-brown door in the narrow street hardly looked like the entrance to a hotel. But, *47, rue Beaunier, Hotel Cecil* it said, on the red blade sign attached to the anonymous, pale-white stucco façade, punched with tiny juliette balconies. It was only a two-star hotel, but it was located within Paris City limits, well-connected by metro and close to the Cité Universitaire, where Anamika's close friends Dinesh and Mohini had spent a brief sabbatical. This proximity to the ghost of their presence had been a comforting thought; she could always call them in the States if she needed an orientation. Besides, it was hard to beat the 60€ per night price Hotel Cecil offered in spite of its convenient location. Anamika stepped inside the tiny foyer after paying off the driver of the Airport Connection, for whom she had waited for over an hour in the drafty morning air, at the Charles de Gaulle passenger pick-up area. Inside, the floor was covered with an elaborate carpet. To one side was a tight lounge with velvety, red love seats and to the other side was an office. An old wooden reception desk stood in the center, next to which a breakfast nook with a selection of teas was also impressively tucked in. A precariously narrow staircase and an equally dangerous-looking elevator appeared to lead up to the five floors of twenty-five rooms the hotel offered. "Bonjour Mademoiselle!" said the thin, well-dressed man at the desk with fanfare, his receding hairline and wiry neck making him look at once distinguished and comical. Anamika was instantly pleased; her travel fatigue evaporated for a moment. This was already the second time she had been addressed as mademoiselle since she had set foot in Paris; the first honor had been conferred by the tardy airport-shuttle driver. Back in America, Anamika was often told she still looked only thirty, but "mademoiselle" was a step up. Politically correct America, especially in Seattle, rarely addressed a woman as "Miss" anymore, and the present regression into traditionalism felt surprisingly pleasant. At least there was some advantage to the pigment in her skin, thought Anamika randomly; it protected her against the crow's feet that had her white counterparts in a dither, feeding the multi-million-dollar skin-care industry. But Anamika's relatives back in Kolkata were of a different ilk; to them it didn't matter how she looked. Her advancing age was a ticking time-bomb, a harbinger of doom for the prospects of marriage and motherhood, both of which were not a woman's prerogative but her obligation. Clicking their tongues against their teeth they talked about her as if she weren't in the room, lamenting in sing-song Bengali, "Eeeesh, more than forty and *still* unmarried? She is getting *so* old, who will marry her now?"

After a few formalities at the reception desk Anamika was handed the key to her room on the third floor. It was attached to a heavy, wooden slat, and she was instructed to turn in the monstrosity to the 24-hour reception desk each time she left the hotel. A porter appeared from somewhere within the office area to help her upstairs with her bags; the elevator seemed to all but fit him and Anamika's rolling suitcase, so she decided to take the stairs. The door to her room opened against the side a full-size bed, as if one were supposed to fall into bed immediately upon unlocking the door, having returned from inebriating forays into the city.

The bedding was adorned by the same cheap, red-velvet she had seen in the foyer downstairs, and even the walls were covered with a peeling, tattered, red-and-gold wallpaper. She squeezed through the narrow gap between the foot of the bed and the wall to inspect the closet-like bathroom. At least it looked thoroughly sanitized, even if in a severely antiseptic, threadbare way. On the wall opposite to the entrance door, a small window opened into some sort of courtyard behind the hotel, and next to the window, a tiny stand held a 27-inch TV. Anamika tipped the porter, struggled to stuff her luggage on one side of the bed, and shut the door. There was nowhere else to go in the room, so she collapsed on the bed, suddenly overcome with sadness and exhaustion. She kicked off her boots, and before she knew it, she was fast asleep.

* * * * *

The liveliness on the street was mesmerizing. Small cars, buses and scooters whizzed by, with the tram moving to its own tune in the generous center of the boulevard. People ambled along on the lavishly wide sidewalks in no apparent hurry, savoring the pleasant Friday twilight. Couples with linked arms stopped to kiss next to the bus-stop, a sign post, or just in the middle of nowhere, their tongues daringly flicking each other with no restraint or inhibition, making Anamika's cheeks flush and groin stir. Back at the hotel she had woken with a start, the gnawing knot in her stomach still intact. The light through the solitary window had indicated it was sometime in the late afternoon; her watch had confirmed 5:12pm. Out of nervous addiction from her business trips, she had turned on her laptop to test Internet connectivity. But the hotel's WiFi hadn't obliged, so she had negotiated her way to the tiny bathroom and taken a quick shower, hoping that the warm water would wash away the cloying depressiveness that clung to her. Then she had picked up a couple of tourist maps and brochures from the hotel foyer, and stepped into the narrow street, instinctively making her way around the corner towards the busy sounds of traffic. She had emerged on Avenue du Général Leclerc, and proceeded to turn another corner on to the broad arterial, Boulevard Jourdan. She had spotted the metro station of Porte d'Orléans at the intersection, and felt the first spark of delight: it was the mouth of the underground that would lead her to the heart of Paris. She couldn't wait to be engulfed by it. Every other storefront slot had seemed to belong either to a flower shop or to a café. Walking a few paces, Anamika had found a crepe stand, and immediately, immense pangs of hunger had sprung from nowhere. She had revived her dormant Indian instincts to jostle with the crowd of people pretending to form a queue, and get in an order of savory crepe with fresh mozzarella, tomatoes and basil. After eating it on the sidewalk, she had stepped into the café with red awnings, taken a seat by its big windows, and ordered a drink that most closely resembled her standard American latte.

Watching the street-side romance, her thoughts migrated to Martin and herself strolling on the sunny, pretty streets of Victoria only two weeks ago. The break-up had been her hardest ever. Martin had made elaborate plans to celebrate her forty-second birthday across the border, booking tickets on the Victoria Clipper and a room in a nice waterfront hotel for three nights. The night before departure, their mid-sized bags packed, they got into the usual argument about Anamika's "unavailability": how she was too busy, how she wasn't fully emotionally involved, how he wanted more, how he wanted to truly be with her. She had experienced that all-too-familiar feeling of claustrophobia, and had spat out the rehearsed response, "I can't do that. I'm not like that." And then, a few seconds later, "I can't do this anymore, Martin; I'm sorry." He had simply stared at her long and hard, and then said gently, "Alright, Anu." It was two in the morning; they had been arguing a while, and the Clipper was scheduled to leave in just a few hours. Anamika had braced for Martin's suggestion to cancel the trip, but he hadn't said a word.

Baffled, she had gone to bed beside him as usual, and the alarm had sounded in three hours. They had called a cab for the brief ride over to the pier, and soon, the speedy boat had whisked them away from Seattle's waterfront to charming Victoria, leaving a foaming trail in the beautiful blue waters.

The three days in Victoria had been the most romantic time she'd ever had with Martin, or for that matter, with anyone else. They had taken leisurely walks along the water, from the Coast Victoria Harbourside hotel, perusing the endless line of boats, and then the street sellers with art, crafts, souvenirs, T-shirts, stones, native jewelry, maple syrup; the list was endless. They had walked all the way from Holland Point Park to Ogden Point, holding hands and strolling down the slim protrusion of land with bright yellow stripes painted down its sides, giving it the perspectival illusion of ending far, far away in the sea. They had made it all the way to the lighthouse at the end, to stare into the big blue of the Straight of Georgia, the wind now nearly blowing them helter-skelter. They had taken a tourist bus to the Butchart gardens, abundant with spring blooms, and Martin had taken spectacular photographs of Anamika at every corner. They had relished three amazing dinners, locking quiet gazes over Spanish food and Greek food and French food. Anamika had experienced bliss, wondering why it couldn't be just this easy all the time. Then they had returned to Seattle, and silently parted ways. Martin had deftly removed all the things that used to lie scattered around her apartment, the sole reminders to her on some weeknights that she had a man in her life. Anamika had been overcome by an unanticipated grief, one she had never felt in all those previous endings, which had been replete with spiraling drama followed by a definitive parting, always to her complete, unequivocal relief. Days later she usually experienced guilt and self-loathing, convinced that something was incorrigibly wrong with her, until this too faded and another man eventually came into her life. Grief was a new, baffling emotion she had never encountered before, and she had no idea what to do with it.

Sipping her coffee and absently perusing the tourist brochures, her thoughts flitted to some of her other lovers. Always, she had reveled in the sensuality, the mystery of an unknown being unraveling to her slowly, through deliberate, energetic sexual exploration, the same way she studied a painting in an art gallery, savored an exquisite delicacy, or took in a vocalist's exploration of a raga at an Indian-classical concert. Note by note she advanced, playing and teasing with the sinuous phrases, surprising with unexpected variations and deviations, lingering and elaborating on special resting points along the way, and moving up the scale towards a crescendo. She enjoyed being the landscape, the instrument, the putty in her lover's hands, and delighted wholeheartedly in returning the favor. She also enjoyed the rich conversation, the good meals, the hikes, theater and music shows, bookstore visits … everything they did together. But she simply couldn't thread these intermittent adventures together to create the demanding continuity commonly associated with being in a relationship, or worse still, with being in love. She cared for her partners; she was happy to see them happy, but she never felt the desire to be attached to them with that distinct, palpable and identified association that so many others seemed to want, even require, for comfort and security. Even as two warm bodies lay spooning, skin touching and breaths mingling, Anamika was curiously aware of being entirely alone in that tiny, fleeting, imperceptible moment before wakefulness slipped into the welcomed unconsciousness of sleep. She had tried to share this observation with her friend from high school, who lived with her husband of fourteen years and two kids back in Kolkata, but Rita had drawn a blank. "You have become *so* American, Anu," she had said after a considered moment. Anamika had flinched; she was frequently reminded that her innate idiosyncrasies were considered so preposterous that they could only be comprehended by well-meaning relatives and friends as negative influences from the West. They simply couldn't fathom that this may just be the way Anamika was; it was too difficult, too challenging to imagine that any normal Indian woman could truly feel like, be like, or live like her. So, they assumed instead that it had to be a compromise, that she was being cheated out of a woman's natural responsibilities and privileges. "No," Anamika had corrected Rita gently, "many American women don't understand me either." But at that moment, little Tutu had come running into his mother's arms crying from a bruised knee, big tears and milky snot mixing into an unhappy mess on his ruddy face, and Anamika had been struck by the realization that there was a gulf much greater and much more insurmountable than the vast oceans between Kolkata and Seattle, which forever separated her from her childhood friend.

Yet there *had* been someone, someone who had understood her only as a like-minded spirit could, someone whose body and hers had danced together in passion and rhythm and freedom from bondage. Anamika had met her all those years ago, on the Delhi University campus, during her undergraduate years. Mala had been a graduate student in economics, older by five years, and so much more directed and postured, her dazzling eyes showcasing her dreams and designs for a fairer, more equitable Indian society. Mala had a room in the WUS Women's hostel, and soon, Anamika had found herself visiting often, mixing chai in small earthen cups and lighting cigarettes, talking for long hours about popular science, politics, and the socio-economic challenges that preoccupied and challenged Mala's brilliant mind. It wasn't clear to Anamika how or when they had become sexual; they had slipped into it seamlessly, ordinarily, obviously. Mala had entered her life in an unexpected and expansive way, pushing and nudging at every corner of her mind and heart, and slowly seeping into her body; she had been shaken out of everything she had been conditioned to believe about love and relationships, and had begun to question, to see, to understand anew. She had seen in front of her, not a man or woman, but a soul, for whom her love was expressed in so many ineffable dimensions. And she had been free to soar in the skies, flying like a bright kite oblivious of the invisible tether that still tied her energetically and unchangeably to Mala. Life had gone on, with Anamika moving to the U.S. for her graduate work, and Mala burying herself inextricably in a rural NGO, but Anamika had never been able to revert to the commonplace, the expected, the societal norm. Now she allowed herself to briefly wonder where Mala was, something she hadn't done in the longest time, something she had shut the door on and hidden away the key, even from herself.

* * * * *

The rapping on the door jolted Anamika out of her sleep, and she sat up like a bolt, rubbing her heavy eyelids in confusion, sinews of dreams floating in red lines in front of her eyes. It took her a few moments to recognize the hotel room, its cheap red envelope closer to orange in the morning light. Assuming it was room service, she pulled on her robe, and poked her sleepy face through a crack in the door, but was greeted with the pearly smile and green eyes of an attractive man. "Hello, Anamika?" he said in a friendly voice and thick French accent, "I am Fabien." Realization began to dawn slowly through the grogginess; she remembered emailing with this friend of her friends, giving him her hotel address so that they could meet up sometime, but never expecting to find him at her door on her first real day in Paris. "Yes, yes," she said, working hard to conceal her rapidly mounting annoyance at this unwelcome eagerness, this tremendous intrusion. "Can you please wait downstairs, and I will meet you there in ten minutes?" "Yes of course," Fabien said generously, unflinching at her terseness. Anamika washed her face, brushed her teeth, and put on some make-up with practiced expertise. She pulled up her long, black curls into a pony-tail, slipped on jeans and a light sweater, tucked her little digital camera in her handbag, and proceeded down the rickety stairs. Fabien was sitting in one of the velvet-covered lounge chairs, sipping coffee from the bar in the breakfast nook. He looked up from the paper in his lap and flashed another smile at Anamika as she stepped off the last stair. She turned in the big wooden key to the man at the reception, and attempted to sound chirpy, "So, do you know a good breakfast place?"

As they walked towards the metro station, Fabien launched into pleasantries; he hoped that she had had a pleasant flight, that she had found some good dinner the previous night, and that the hotel was comfortable; he had called and left her a message the night before saying he'd be there to pick her up at nine in the morning. *So he hadn't been entirely mannerless*, Anamika thought, *just presumptuous*. Fabien ushered her through the metro entrance, and slipped her a weekend pass. Anamika was now more surprised and curious than annoyed, studying him sideways to take in his handsome features, and wondering why he was acting like her appointed host. Had Dinesh and Mohini said something to him? They hadn't told her much about Fabien, just that he was a post-doc in the Math department, lived not too far away from Hotel Cecil, and would be happy to help her out if she needed it. Anamika had been grateful, and had established contact with him via e-mail, and then promptly forgotten all about it. And here they were, already off to breakfast together.

They emerged from the underground on Quai d'Orsay by the Seine, and Anamika's spirits lifted. The food at Café de l'Alma was outstanding. They ate elaborately, and chatted well into the noon hour, Anamika's initial recalcitrance having rapidly worn off in the charming surroundings and Fabien's warm company. She surprised herself by telling him quite a bit about her life in the States, her work-related travels and demanding clients, and even bits and pieces about her days of schooling in Kolkata and college in Delhi. He, on the other hand, remained reticent, making only passing references to his college days in Versailles, preferring instead to inquire after and listen intently to Anamika's stories. Having learned of her cultivated interest in buildings from her work in business development for an international architectural firm, he promised to point out some of the modern architectural delights of Paris.

They ventured east, past the Notre Dame and the fork in the Seine to the Arab World Institute, a jewel of a building designed by Jean Nouvel. The breathtaking façade of moving geometric motifs in metal that acted as brise soleil, looked like a giant, but intricately woven Persian rug. They stepped inside to briefly experience the interior spaces bathed in filtered light, reminding Anamika anachronistically of the marble lattices in Salim Chisti's tomb in Fatehpur Sikri. They strolled back along the river, and crossed its southern fork over to the Notre Dame, its exquisite rose windows also glorious as passageways of light, inspiration and divinity. People milled about in huge numbers, birds flocked, photographers clicked, musicians played, artists drew. Fabien led Anamika further north, a quiet rapport already growing between them as only among old friends, with Fabien occasionally speaking up to point to this or that sight. The metal guts of the famous and controversial Pompidou center appeared without warning, and Fabien looked delighted with Anamika's surprise as they explored the building, a rebellious, iconoclastic statement from the late seventies. From here, Fabien pointed towards the hill of Montmartre, and the Basilica of the Sacré Cœur on its summit, and Anamika instantly felt an inexplicable, magnetic draw towards this ancient artists' haven.

By now Anamika's legs had begun to quiver with fatigue, so they took the metro towards the gardens of the Louvre, and sat down on a park bench with coffees and croissants in hand from a nearby vendor. The plaza of the Louvre was still full of people in the fading afternoon light, and the metal-and-glass pyramidal entrances designed by I.M. Pei glowed warmly in the center, acting like purposeful but elegant contradictions to the ancient, majestic architecture of the museum building. Anamika vowed to return here the next day to spend most of it in the Louvre, to enjoy in solitude its world-famous, priceless collection.

* * * * *

She peeked over and in between at least forty shoulders in her line-of-sight, to catch incomplete, unsatisfactory glimpses of the Mona Lisa. Anamika had spent more than two hours in the Sully wing with Egyptian, Etruscan, Middle Eastern, Greek and Roman antiques, and painting after painting of medieval art with bright, voluptuous women, muscular men, clouds and winged angels. She had finally arrived in the room with the Renaissance masterpiece the world has lauded for more than five hundred years, and to her annoyance, couldn't manage a clear view. She was surprised at how small the painting really was, and with its cordoned off security enclosure, the product of Da Vinci's prescience appeared now as a sorry victim of humanity's inherent frailties. Anamika inched her way through the crowd, determined to not leave without viewing the painting as intimately as possible. She stared into the eyes of this much-talked-about but little-known woman, and the mysterious and enigmatic smile cast a spell on her. She stood there, just staring, until the jostling crowd snapped her back into reality, and she waded through it again to exit the room.

Anamika had risen relatively early to get to the Louvre as soon as it opened, picking up a crepe and coffee from the stand near Hotel Cecil for breakfast. She hadn't felt too hungry after another elaborate, leisurely dinner Fabien and she had enjoyed the night before at a beautiful riverside restaurant. Afterwards, he had suggested a visit to the Eiffel Tower. "The crowds and lines are a lot smaller in the evening, and the tower is open until midnight!" he had said, the smile in his lovely green eyes already familiar and comforting to Anamika. And indeed, the tower's nighttime ambience had been spectacular, the metalwork enhanced by sparkling bursts of white light from computer-controlled light projectors and strobe lights. They had taken the elevator all the way to the top, enjoying the cool evening breeze and the floodlit bridges, churches, and other landmarks in the glittering Parisian nightscape. Later he had walked her to the hotel from the metro station, leaning forward to kiss her cheek in the red foyer, and Anamika had flushed at how pleasant the attention felt even though she knew it was common French courtesy on his part. "Goodnight," he had said simply, "See you in the evening tomorrow." Fabien had to get some work done during the day on Sunday, he had explained, but had promised to meet her for dinner. Anamika was surprised that her initial annoyance at the prospect of a stranger suffocating her introspective time in Paris had so quickly transformed into a longing for his company.

Now she was wading through sculptures in Richelieu, the ground floor of the museum, but finding herself quickly losing interest. Thoughts of Martin were popping up in her head again, distracting her, tugging at her stomach. She left the building and strolled into the plaza, enjoying the warmth of the sun on her skin, and the sight of so many people simply sitting around the fountains, or leaning against the glass of the pyramids. She reflected on the contrast with America, where the absence of any space, any silence between activities, stuff and to-dos had created an addictive pace of life. Similar to what she felt here, she was aware of a certain peacefulness on her visits to India; in spite of the screaming intensity and utter mayhem, or perhaps because of these, there was a curious slowing down of time, a relinquishing of all control over individual destiny, making her float along in communion with the masses. And within this floating and drifting, which paradoxically also afforded a heightened awareness, from time to time opened a secret door to inner calm and tranquility, something she could only experience in tiny, bite-size bits, before her mind returned to its frenetic, maniacal racing all over again. She felt that same door opening now, as she walked down the legendary Champs Elysées, with its generous breadth and its handsome, clipped chestnut trees. Fabien had told her that the French called it *la plus belle avenue du monde*, which translated to "the most beautiful avenue in the world." She could see why. A mile or so into it Anamika came upon the section lined with cinemas, cafés and luxury specialty shops that made this the most expensive strip of real estate in all of Europe. She stepped in and out of the stores, feeling silken fabrics, touching leather, watching people. She just loved the people. She walked into a small café, and ordered a ham sandwich in a delicious, flaky croissant, eating it slowly and deliberately with awareness of every bite. Inspired by Fabien, she also ordered a dark espresso instead of her usual milky coffee, stirred in a teaspoon of sugar, and slurped it down like she had seen him do. She smiled at the shock of the bittersweet liquid, the smooth feeling of it on her tongue making her imagine how his tongue might feel on hers.

Back on the street she continued to walk westwards, past the barricade of potted flowers that marked the outdoor seating of the famous Fouquet's café, where she was to meet Fabien at seven in the evening. She arrived at the majestic Arc de Triomphe, pensively studied the Napoleonic monument for a while and then, on a whim, remembering the draw she had felt towards Montmartre, she darted underground to head north-east. Once there, she found the artists' plaza, and strolled through all the portraits in progress – frozen moments of feeling in charcoal – the swish-swish movements of the soft graphite as pleasant as the gentle afternoon breeze. An old, hapless woman beckoned her with persistent, pleading gestures, and the desperation in the woman's eyes forced Anamika to oblige. As she drew her subject, the woman looked up and giggled periodically, as if with maternal affection for Anamika's youthful beauty, her shrunken eyes twinkling with mischief as she made wide motions on rough, gray parchment. An hour later, Anamika had in her hands an impression of herself that made her look sixteen again, and she willingly parted with the 40€ the old woman was asking.

* * * * *

Two nubile, slender women with small breasts were pole-dancing back-to-back on the tiny stage, dropping their scanty garments one by one, occasionally turning towards each other to smile and touch and fondle. Once they left the stage, naked and arm-in-arm, a man and a woman walked on from opposite corners, bowed, and looked Anamika straight in the eye. She felt entirely disembodied, as if it were not she but someone she was observing, who had walked into this glitzy building in Pigalle.

It had been about four o'clock when the old woman had finished her portrait, and with three more hours in hand before she needed to meet Fabien back on Avenue des Champs Elysées, Anamika had suddenly remembered wanting to see the Moulin Rouge. Wandering down the row of strip clubs and sex shops, she had stopped in front of this multi-story storefront, with provocative, luring life-size mannequins and show-box images in its upper windows, and with big, electrified red letters that said: SEXODROME. She hadn't been able to help but peep behind the heavy, black drapes at street level. Once past her initial trepidation of looking in, she had stepped inside gingerly, and found herself surrounded with the largest collection of sex objects and toys she could ever have imagined. People – couples and individuals alike – were perusing the various offerings as if they might be examining apples and avocados in a grocery store. For background cheer, looping videos of screaming, orgasmic duos and multiples were running on wall-mounted screens in the four corners.

Quickly growing intrepid, Anamika had launched a thorough investigation of the various packages. Twenty minutes later, feeling like a giddy schoolgirl, she had stepped up to the counter with a pink, pocket-size "bullet" and an alarmingly large, two-pronged, motorized plastic phallus. Making her first ever purchase of sex-toys, she had searched the face of the man at the check-out counter for any lurking judgment, but he had smiled brightly and said, "Live sex show for you, mademoiselle?" Before she knew it, she had parted with yet another 40€ and allowed herself to be ushered into a small auditorium with raunchy, red-velvet seats, sofas and benches arranged around a tiny, rotating stage. She had imagined that she'd been seated early for the show and other patrons would be arriving shortly. But then the music had begun to play, and she had realized that no one else was coming; they were running the show just for her. Her stomach had turned in fear. She had considered bolting through the closed auditorium door and running out of the building, but instead she had sat clutching the slipping velvet drape on her chair, waiting to see what would happen next. She was glued to a train wreck.

Now the man and woman were fully naked, the music was intensifying, and the disco lights at the edge of the stage were shooting pulsating beams of color at the two bodies tugging, poking, grabbing, and fondling each other on the bare floor. The room was so small and the seats so close together, that Anamika thought she could touch them with the slightest forward motion. With nobody else in the audience, she had none of the convenient obscurity and anonymity a crowd afforded, and now it felt as if she were herself on display, fooled into sharing the stage with the two performers, roped into nonconsensual intimacy with the two strangers. At one point they took a brief pause for the man to perfunctorily unwrap and slip on a condom; then they resumed their advancing foreplay and transitioned to copulation. Anamika's cheeks flamed and her stomach made a tight fist, but her groin was moist and pulsing in total, brazen contradiction of her mind's sensibilities.

The couple made periodic, purposeful eye-contact with her, and eventually she was compelled to surrender her fears and gaze into their faces, studying their expressions as they progressed towards some semblance of a finale. The woman, probably in her forties like Anamika but with straggly brown-blond hair and lines of aging criss-crossing her face, wore a passionless and apathetic expression, or perhaps it was an expression of loneliness. Could she be enjoying *any* of this? Anamika dared to ask herself. The dark-haired man looked younger; his eyes were closed, his faraway expression revealed a practiced, psychological distance from the actual act, to focus on an isolated physical stimulation; he too was terribly, undeniably alone. Was *he* enjoying this? He finished with a mellow grunt, and before Anamika could even shift in her seat, they bounced up to standing, turned to each other for a quick, professional kiss as if to simply say "thank you," and then held hands to courtesy to their sole audience member, entirely unperturbed by their stark nakedness. Anamika nodded to them, suddenly overcome with a mix of sadness, warmth and gratitude for these two strangers, who had bared their bodies for her benefit and displayed to her the most stripped-down, unglamorous, naked reality of the human condition: ten minutes of fluid release that had the power to put flesh on sale, to cause intrigue and crime, to wield hurt and devastation, but also to create new life. Was this how Anamika and a partner might look in bed to a hovering onlooker, while within her fertile imagination and insatiable sensuality, she told herself stories of rich, complex, never-ending discoveries? Is this the truth she had spent the last twenty years running away from?

* * * * *

They stood facing each other, yet again, in the red foyer of Hotel Cecil. Dinner at Fouquet's had been delightful, surrounded by vibrant groups of people, and the elegance of leather banquettes and rattan furniture. Anamika had ordered a delicious, melting-in-the-mouth chicken, slow-cooked in a wine reduction, and had described her day to Fabien, judiciously omitting the two hours in Pigalle. She had wanted to lean forward, smile into his eyes and say, "You will be proud of me. Today I saw both ends of the spectrum of art: high art and low art." Or better still, "I saw Truth. Not in a temple or a monastery, but in a live sex show." Now, standing in the hotel foyer, again she wanted to lean towards him, this time to touch his brow and jaw, to nuzzle his neck, to kiss the slender mouth that had charmed her with dazzling smiles all weekend. By the expression in his eyes she knew it would be easy, too easy, to lead him up the creaky stairs. Instead, she stayed firm on her feet, and allowed him to bend and kiss her cheek like he had the night before. "Goodbye, Anu," he said, lingering, "It was very nice knowing you. I very much hope you will stay in touch. Please say my hello to Dinesh and Mohini."

She ran up the stairs to her room, and quickly shut the door. Landing hard on the bed, she turned out her handbag and emptied its contents: wallet, passport, phone, sunglasses, camera, hairbrush, and from underneath all this, the bag of goodies she had acquired from the Sexodrome. She unwrapped the large, unwieldy object, lay back, and allowed herself to submit to the quietly whirring phallus between her legs, melting into its caresses, rocking to its gyrations. Self-pleasure was intimately known to Anamika from as long back as she could remember, but this was about self-empowerment. It was an arrival at no-seeking; she had wandered, searched, and explored, but ultimately, she had found the entire universe in her own core. She knew at last to not run away, to become one with herself.

Gratitude

I humbly thank all those with whom I have crossed paths in life's journey, interactions with whom and windows into whose experiences are the genesis of these stories. While the central ideas in these narratives are biographical, they should be read as fiction.

This book is lovingly dedicated to the late Meenakshi Mukherjee, renowned literary critic and author, (but simply "mashi" to me), who took precious time out of the last year of her richly productive life to read my work, give me feedback, and encourage me to publish. Her voice grew stronger in her sudden and shocking absence, and I was compelled to complete and publish this humble collection.

I am grateful to Seth Godin for his book Linchpin; Seth reminded me just when I needed it that "shipping" work so it can touch others is what completes an artist. I am grateful to my esteemed Guru, Pandita Tripti Mukherjee, for her incredible gift of music, and blessings that anything is possible.

My special gratitude is due to Shirin Subhani and Naveen Valluri for their generosity in supporting the publishing and distribution effort, to Tiyash Bandyopadhyay for her help with marketing and promotion, and to Shirin and Parijat Nandi for copy-editing and proof-reading; all shortcomings in the book are, of course, solely mine. I am also grateful to Bidisha Ghosh, Shirin, and Tiyash for reading my stories in their incipient forms and giving me valuable feedback.

In times of uncertain seeking and random creative muses, for their love, inspiration, encouragement, partnership, guidance, or support, my heartfelt gratitude goes to Janice Adams, Saara Ahmed, Sabina Ansari,

Sana Ashraf, Trisha Barua, Manoj Biswas, Rudrajit (Atom) Bose, Devasmita Chakraverty, Priyam Das, Ranu Dattagupta, Sharmishtha Dattagupta, Sushanta Dattagupta, Bonnie Duncan, Scott Francis, Elizabeth Friesen, David Gibson, Nilima Ghosh, Preeti Ghosh, Rabindra Ghosh, Rupamanjari Ghosh, Indrani Goyal, Amita Gupta, Robb Hamilton, Srivani Jade, Agastya Kohli, Sandeep Krishnamurty, Archana Kumar, Meg Lee, Amrita Madan, Alexi Marmot, Robert Mankin, Andrew McCune, Rita Meher, Rodger Messer, Larry Miggins, Bipasha Mukherjee, Rohini Mukherjee, Sangeeta Naidu, Raman Narayanan, Farah Nousheen, Arshiya Qadri, Nitika Raj, Meenakshi Rishi, Meg Ryan, Shaline Samy, Kate Sluyter, Megan Strawn, Checha Sokolovic, Trisna Tanus, Jay and Schuyler Thoman, Ruchita Varma, Rachael Victoria, Jonathan Ward, Jason Week, Tully Wehr, Anya Woestwin, and my friends, readers and supporters at Bloggermoms, Chaya, and Tasveer.

And finally, my thanks to incredible Lailah; as Dr. Bernie Siegel has said: to err is human, to forgive is feline.

About the Author

Photograph: Jason J. Week

Shahana Dattagupta lives and writes in Seattle. She also sings and teaches Hindustani classical music, produces visual art, acts in local theater productions (in Hindi and English), and consults in architectural and communication design. (She hopes that the Renaissance person is not extinct.) Shahana was born in the United States and raised in various parts of India. She returned to her country of birth for graduate school and work. 2010 is her thirteenth year in America, so it is, naturally, an auspicious year for the publication of her first book.

LaVergne, TN USA
17 February 2011
216938LV00005B/265/P